Leonard Everett Fisher, painter, illustrator, author, and educator, was born and raised in New York City. His formal art training began at the Heckscher Foundation in 1932 and was completed, after his wartime military service, at the Yale Art School, from which he received a Master of Fine Arts degree and the Winchester Fellowship. He had studied previously with Moses Soyer, Reginald Marsh, Olindo Ricci, and Serge Chermayeff. In 1950 Mr. Fisher received a Pulitzer Art Fellowship. He spent much of that year in Europe, returning home in 1951 to become dean of the Whitney School of Art in New Haven, Connecticut. He resigned from that post in 1953 and turned his attention to children's literature. Since then he has illustrated approximately two hundred children's books, about thirty of which he has written, including *The Death of "Evening Star."* He has received numerous citations, and in 1968 he was awarded the Premio Grafico for juvenile illustration by the International Book Fair, Bologna, Italy—the only American thus honored. Books containing his illustrations have been published in a variety of foreign languages and distributed throughout the world by the United States Information Agency. In addition he has designed ten United States postage stamps. Mr. and Mrs. Fisher live in Westport, Connecticut.

Leonard Everett Fisher

A Novel About Baseball,
ESP, and Time Warps

DOUBLEDAY & COMPANY, INC., GARDEN CITY, NEW YORK

Library of Congress Cataloging in Publication Data

Fisher, Leonard Everett.
  Noonan.

  SUMMARY: A knock on the head with a baseball
catapults a young baseball player one hundred years into the
future to the year 1996.
  [1. Baseball—Fiction.   2. Space and time—Fiction]
I. Title.
PZ7.F533No   [Fic]
ISBN: 0-385-11692-6 Trade
       0-385-11693-4 Prebound
Library of Congress Catalog Card Number 77–80887

AUTHOR'S NOTE

The story you are about to read is ridiculous. It never happened. Or did it? Or could it? Most of the leading characters you will meet are absolutely fictitious. I invented them. Perhaps it is the other way around—they invented me and I am their instrument. No matter. Some of the characters in the book are very real or were very real:

Mayor Seth Low, for example, long ago mayor of the city of Brooklyn and of the city of New York, President Emeritus of Columbia University, and a fine New Yorker in every respect.

The Van Siclens of Brooklyn, early settlers and outstanding citizens.

The 1896 Cincinnati Red Stockings, Joe DiMaggio, Tom Seaver, Johnny Bench, Jerry Koosman, and others—gentlemen all and all a credit to their profession.

In the interest of the narrative, the appearance, behavior, and conversation of these very real personages bear little resemblance to actuality—their nature, deeds, and legends. Should these matters bear such resemblance, it would not only be coincidental, it would be a shocking revelation of the indisputable truth of extrasensory perception and other psychic phenomenon.

L.E.F.

Westport, Conn.
1978

I.

Time is a clock on the wall
or nothing at all.
Time is for dreaming
or scheming.
Time is the umpire's call:
"Foul ball!"

1.

1896. This was to be the year of destiny for the Brooklyn Dutchmen Professional Baseball Club. The team was one of nine clubs that made up the financially faltering Continental League.

This was to be the year the Dutchmen would unleash their spectacular fifteen-year-old pitcher, Johnny Noonan, and inflict him on all of baseball. In the mind of Charles Patrick O'Brien, owner and manager, Johnny Noonan's pitching talent was the lever for unseating the National League's domination of organized baseball.

"There's got to be two major leagues," Charlie would lecture his fellow owners. "And it has got to be us, the Continentals, who give the Nationals a run for their money!"

More than that, however, and deep in his consciousness, Charlie O'Brien wanted nothing more than to clobber the Cincinnati Red Stockings, the first and slickest club in baseball. The two teams had never played each other.

Worse still, his chief competitor on his home turf was another Brooklyn ball club who cast their lot with the powerful National League a few years back. In all fairness, Charlie O'Brien had been offered the opportunity of joining the National League first. But he balked. He claimed the ten-dollar fee was too steep for such a chancy venture.

9

Anyway, by the looks of it and at the moment, the Dutchmen's future was shaky. And the Continental League's prospects for survival were even shakier: Johnny Noonan stopped a foul-line drive with his head while waiting his turn to bat during a preseason exhibition game in Baltimore.

"Foul ball!" cried Studs Rosencranz, the gargantuan umpire, as Johnny fell like a rock. "Three and two."

The three thousand fans who paid thirty-five cents each to sit behind a rope on some rickety bleachers groaned.

"You jerk," screamed O'Brien at Big Jack Eastman, his batter. "You've just cost us the season!"

Big Jack looked over at the unconscious form of Johnny Noonan spread-eagled about fifty feet from home plate. He seemed to shrink as the calamity settled on him. Charlie O'Brien walked past the knot of players that quickly collected around his star pitcher and began to circle Eastman.

"You big gorilla. Look what you've done!"

"It was an accident, boss. You'd think I meant to kill the kid. He threw me a strike right down the middle. I had to swing to stay alive."

Eastman had a sinking sensation that his choice of words, "to stay alive," was somehow inappropriate.

"Yeah. Sure. A strike. Hey, Studs," O'Brien called to the umpire, "what was it?"

"A ball. Ball four is what it should have been. High and inside."

O'Brien quit his endless circling and turned on Eastman. His huge mustache twitched convulsively over a craggy face now warped with rage. O'Brien was never much to look at anyway. But at the moment he was even worse looking than usual—the nearest thing to a screeching man-eating gargoyle. Eastman, who towered over the short, barrel-chested manager, wanted no part of him. He backed off holding his

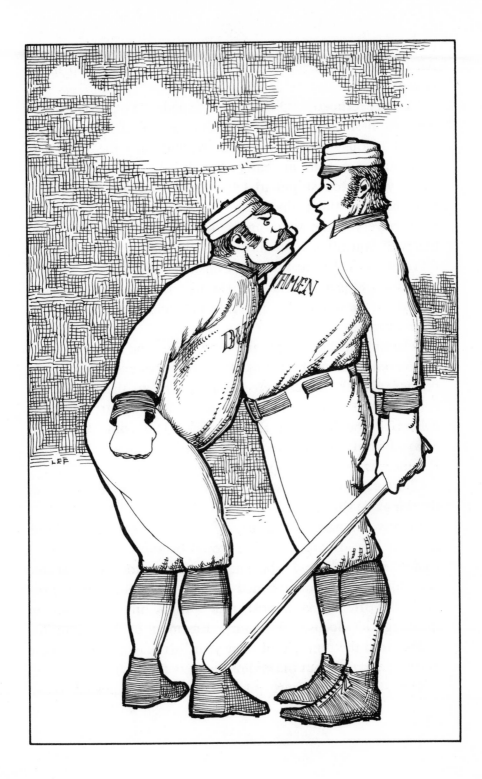

bat at arm's length to keep O'Brien a safe distance away. All the while he kept looking for Rosencranz to step in between.

"You beerhead," O'Brien continued. "You could have been on first base. A free ride. But no! You had to swing late at a lousy ball and knock the kid into the middle of next year—or into an early grave! You got suckered because you're too stupid to tell a ball from a strike. And I lost the best thing that ever happened to this club. The kid'll never be the same again, provided he lives. And neither will you after I get through with you. You're still alive all right, Jack. But just barely. Consider that!"

O'Brien lunged for the bat. He missed. Eastman had flung it aside as he found Rosencranz and ducked behind the very wide umpire.

O'Brien had his say for the time being and marched back to the still prostrate form of Johnny Noonan, his young pitcher. Chunks of ice were being applied to the left side of Johnny's head. An ambulance was on its way. Its clattering bell could be heard in the distance. The game would be delayed until Johnny Noonan was "in the meat wagon," as Rosencranz put it, and removed from the field.

Charles P. O'Brien was absolutely right about some of the things he shrieked.

Johnny Noonan would never be the same again. True. But just how different Johnny would become, O'Brien in his wildest dreams could not imagine. True, too, he lost the best thing that ever happened to the club—but only temporarily. O'Brien was almost right when, in a manner of speaking, he accused Big Jack Eastman of knocking the pitcher into the "middle of next year." It was not the middle of next year at all but the end of the next century!

The still unconscious pitcher was gently placed on a

12

stretcher and lifted into the ambulance—a horse-drawn wagon emblazoned on both its black sides with the words

AMBULANCE
CITY OF BALTIMORE, MD.

in gold leaf.

The driver yelled, "Giddyap."

Rosencranz bellowed, "Play ball!"

Big Jack Eastman stepped up to the plate ready to redeem himself. A great chorus of boos surged over him as he steadied his bat. The count was still three and two.

"Uncle Robbie" Robinson, the Baltimore catcher, smashed his fist into his mitt and looked up at Eastman.

"Who's next, Jack? How 'bout O'Brien?"

Big Jack turned his head and snarled at Uncle Robbie just as the ball sizzled over the plate, waist-high.

"Strike three. Yer out," Rosencranz screamed in Big Jack's ear.

Big Jack Eastman had been suckered again.

Johnny Noonan was not born with a baseball in his hand no matter what Charles Patrick O'Brien liked people to think. No, not exactly. Perhaps a sea shell or two would be more like it.

Johnny Noonan quietly arrived into the world in one of the upstairs rooms of his parents' loud saloon—Mike and

Elsie's Paradise Alley. The place was a gawdy establishment in the heart of Brooklyn's playland-by-the-sea, Coney Island.

Mike and Elsie Noonan were proud of their saloon, festooned as it was with great, tinkly chandeliers, endless mirrors in swirling gold frames, and cheap but expensive-looking bric-a-brac. Here, at Noonans' Paradise Alley, draught beer and Irish whiskey flowed as copiously as the Atlantic Ocean tides washed the nearby five-mile stretch of beach.

Most of the clientele, men and women alike, were non-swimming fashion plates who spilled over from the neighboring Brighton Race Track. Once in a while, Brooklyn's own much beloved reforming politician, Mayor Seth Low, in a mood to spread his goodness all over scandal-ridden Coney Island, would walk into the saloon trailed by an assortment of mean-looking Brooklyn detectives.

"I'll have a root beer, Elsie," he would call out. Then he would launch into his favorite theme: why Brooklyn deserved to remain an independent city and not be swallowed up by that sinful place across the river, New York.

"It was here on our sandy beach, on our Coney Island, in the year 1609," the mayor would begin, "that Henry Hudson first set foot on this continent. Here on this Brooklyn beach began the history of New York. From here that fabled explorer sailed through the Narrows and up the North River—naming the latter after himself, Hudson's River."

Everyone cheered.

"And need I remind you that General Washington gathered his army of ten thousand on Brooklyn Heights to meet the British challenge?"

"But he got beat!" someone boomed from the rear of the saloon.

"Throw the bum out," someone else yelled. "Let the mayor go on."

The mayor went on, unruffled.

"And need I remind you that ever since the days of Tom Jefferson's presidency we have been the home of one of the wonders of the maritime world? The Brooklyn Naval Shipyard!"

Another cheer.

"You are right to cheer, my friends. *Our* Navy Yard gave the Union in the awful War Between the States the *Monitor*, the first iron-clad naval vessel. She changed the course of naval history."

"She sure did," that same someone boomed from the rear of the saloon. "She sank!"

"Throw the bum out!"

Mike Noonan personally sorted out the crowd in the rear and flung the culprit onto the street and into the arms of a burly policeman. The policeman dragged the man off to the Eighth Street Precinct, where he was slapped into a cell for disturbing the peace.

Mayor Low, still unruffled, continued.

"And what about our neighbor, New York City?"

"What about New York?" the saloon crowd wanted to know.

"A municipality of crime and degeneration," the mayor answered, conveniently overlooking the plain fact that peaceful, bucolic Brooklyn was not far behind; a state of affairs —Brooklyn affairs—that he, Seth Low, was trying to correct.

"Crime and degeneration," he repeated. "I'll have another root beer, Elsie. Crime and degeneration," he exclaimed once more for emphasis and then added, "five minutes from dissolution; five minutes from bankruptcy; five minutes from Judgment Day."

Here and there a number of heavy-lidded patrons took out their timepieces to watch the minute hand approach New York's doomsday. The mayor's second mug of root

16

beer came sliding down the long wet bar counter as if it were shot out of a cannon. It left a wake of slippery white foam the entire length of the bar. Mike Noonan deftly grabbed the mug and personally delivered it to the mayor.

"Thank you, Mike. You are a fine man. I tell you one and all, my friends, that New York citizens are fleeing in every direction to escape the leaden hand of political corruption, fiscal ruin, and all manner of deprivation. And most of them are emigrating to our fair city of Brooklyn."

Another cheer went up with such force that it shook the glassy chandeliers and sent waves of tinkly sounds from one end of the saloon to the other. Usually, that was Seth Low's signal to depart and spread his political reforming gospel elsewhere. Little did he realize that before the century would end—on New Year's Day, 1898—Brooklyn would be annexed by the city of New York to become a mere borough; and that he, Seth Low, three years after that would become mayor of "Greater New York."

Seth Low would reach the summit of New York politics in the very same year—1901—that a new major baseball league, the American League, would rise to challenge successfully the National League's strangle hold on organized baseball. All the other leagues, associations, and independent clubs would fade away—the Federal League, the Union and Western Associations—all of them. Even the Brooklyn Dutchmen and their Continental League would pass into oblivion.

Of course, none of this had much to do with Johnny Noonan presently lying in a Baltimore hospital bed with a fractured skull. Except for one small, almost forgotten connection, that is.

Once Mayor Low, on the verge of departing Mike and Elsie's Paradise Alley saloon, turned to his applauding audience, remarking, "This city of Brooklyn needs something better than a gambler's race track to put her on the map. You know it. I know it. And the Good Lord knows we belong on the map for the whole world to see."

A great cheer echoed around the saloon.

"Another root beer, Mr. Mayor?"

"No, not now, Elsie, my dear. I must shortly return to the burdens of my office. What Brooklyn needs is something to represent the high purpose of her people and the body and soul of our glorious country."

"What Brooklyn needs, Mr. Mayor, is a first-class professional baseball club."

"The gentleman is right! What is your name, friend?"

"Charles Patrick O'Brien, sir."

"Mr. O'Brien, that is just what I had in mind."

Charlie O'Brien had had it in mind for years.

"We should form a club," Mayor Low went on, "with the best players we can find. Money should be no obstacle. And then we should challenge the Cincinnatis. That would do it, don't you think? That would put us—our fair city—on the map."

The mayor surveyed his audience now feverish with the future. The murmuring of the crowd rose to a riotous din as the excitement of Seth Low's proposal quickened everyone's pulse. And as the patrons of Paradise Alley throbbed with visions of fame and glory, a faint smile creased the mayor's handsome face.

Mayor Seth Low knew what he was talking about. No one became someone until they beat the Cincinnati Red Stockings. They may have fallen on hard times, still they were the aristocrats of baseball. The management of the Cincinnati Red Stockings was the first to pay its players for playing baseball. That made the "Reds" the first professional team in baseball. They had seniority forever—or at least as long as they remained a baseball club. They even

18

played ball on Sundays—for money—and no one complained.

The mayor was even more shrewd than he let on. Cincinnati, the glamour team, was a sitting duck. They had already begun to lose a few ball games, proving, naturally, that they could be beaten. Moreover, once they had been kicked out of the National League for one reason or another and teetered on the edge of another league before returning to the Nationals. They were vulnerable. But more importantly, Seth Low wanted to demonstrate that the city of Brooklyn in the state of New York was indeed a full-fledged city and not an appendage of Manhattan Island—a lost cause, to be sure (as events later proved)—nevertheless, a worthy cause.

The mayor could not risk a challenge to New York City. What if the Brooklyn team should lose? The humiliation would be devastating. Eternal. Not even time would heal the gaping wound like it heals most other things. The people of Brooklyn would wear the disgrace—and that is what it would be—disgrace—forever. The mayor's own ambitions would be immobilized. His career would turn to ashes. All would be lost. Down the drain.

But—what if Brooklyn should challenge Cincinnati to a ball game? By going right to the top, ignoring Manhattan Island completely, Brooklynites would show their contempt for New Yorkers; their independent strain; their big-league status; and their big-city status—all at the same time. The people of Brooklyn would humble their neighbors on the other side of the East River. Win or lose, there could be no disgrace in any of it. And no one's career would go down the drain.

"Oh, wonder of wonders," mused Mayor Seth Low.

"Sleep on that, ladies and gentlemen, sleep on that," he told them. "But do not oversleep."

19

3.

"What do you make of all that, Mike?"

"I don't know, Charlie. The mayor is a clever man—a good man."

"What does that have to do with anything? What does he know about baseball?"

"Nothing, I suppose. Or next to nothing. Politics. That's his game. Politics. And I don't think baseball and politics were meant for each other."

"Maybe so," mused Charlie O'Brien, twisting and caressing his great mustache. "But I'll tell you one thing, my friend: Right now they are one and the same thing. Put it all together—baseball and politics—and it spells *m-o-n-e-y,* money—money enough to bank-roll a team. And the mayor is just in the proper mood to steer me in the right direction. I mean to have a team, and at the moment our good Mayor Low is the key to my success. Just you wait and see."

Charlie and Mike Noonan were at the beach. Young Johnny was with them. It was a warm, breezeless middle autumn morning and much too warm for this time of year. The sun had passed the equator on its southern trek weeks ago but summer lingered on—Indian summer. Here and there a few people wandered up and down the vast expanse of sand in an aimless, dreamy journey.

The Atlantic Ocean was calm and flat as far as the eye could see, a steely bluish gray under the morning sun. The distant Jersey shore and Sandy Hook were a wavering haze on the horizon.

Charlie, Mike, and Johnny tried to skim clam shells over the water as they chatted and dodged the outgoing tide weakly lapping at their feet. Charlie never missed. Every one of his clam shells skipped four or five times along the water's surface before stopping and sinking. Mike was not too bad at it. He managed to make every other snow-white shell skip along the water a few times. Johnny had no luck at all. He was just a baby who had only learned to walk a year or two ago, let alone learn to throw. He simply picked up whatever was nearby and flung it at the water—shells, rocks, sand, dead crabs—it did not matter. Whatever he hurled did not go very far and promptly sank where it hit.

"Here, let me show you how to do that, Johnny," O'Brien offered.

O'Brien found a good-size shell, hefted it for a second in his meaty hand, and then crooked his thick index finger firmly around one curved edge. Satisfied with the feel of his grip, O'Brien whipped the shell at the water with a slightly sidearm, slightly underhand motion. The white missile soared gently upward at first, leveled off, dipped, touched the water, bounced, touched the water a few more times, bounced a few more times, and finally settled lazily about fifty yards out.

"There. How did you like that? Now it's your turn."

Johnny dug into the sand and found a shell much larger than his small hand. Quickly, he hurled it at the water. It barely reached the water's edge some three feet away. There it was picked up by the outgoing sea wash and disappeared from sight.

"Not bad, my boy. Not bad," O'Brien laughed. "You've got possibilities. You'll be my pitcher someday."

4.

Johnny Noonan grew tall and bony on the beach at Coney Island, learning to skim snow-white clam shells along the water and out of sight. And this he did with long arms, big hands, appealing sidearm grace, and constant accuracy. By the time Johnny had mastered the art of seaside shell skimming, Charlie O'Brien had himself a losing, but experienced, ball team—the Brooklyn Dutchmen. And just as he had predicted, Mayor Seth Low had been the key to it all.

O'Brien had little difficulty approaching the mayor with his baseball dream. One afternoon, not long after Mayor Low had excited the patrons of Paradise Alley with his baseball notion, Charlie walked into the mayor's offices in downtown Brooklyn and announced himself.

"Charles Patrick O'Brien to see the mayor."

"What is your business, Mr. O'Brien? And whom do you represent?" the mayor's secretary wanted to know.

"My business is baseball, madam," replied Charlie in a manner resembling an ambassador at the royal court of Queen Victoria. "I represent the desires of the people of the city of Brooklyn in the Empire State of New York."

The secretary was unmoved by Charlie O'Brien's tone and posture. "Is the mayor expecting you?" she demanded. "My date book shows no appointment for you."

"Madam, I have no appointment," Charlie responded in his best grand style. "But I think the mayor will see me."

The secretary gave Charlie a "we-shall-see-about-that" look and marched off to consult with Mayor Low. She re-

23

turned a few minutes later to escort Charles Patrick O'Brien into the mayor's private office. As she left, closing the door behind her, Charlie gave her an "I-told-you-so" look.

"Ah. Mr. O'Brien. How nice to see you again." Seth Low was always genuinely anxious to see everyone again. "I had a feeling you would come by to see me on a matter of mutual interest. Shall we discuss the future of Brooklyn baseball?"

The mayor seemed to have nothing pressing on his calendar. He devoted the next hour to an exchange of broad ideas about baseball. There were more meetings between the two over the next several months. Charlie enjoyed the discussions and his growing friendship with so eminent a figure as Mayor Seth Low. Yet, he felt he was no closer to forming a baseball team than before he knew the mayor. Frustrated, he decided to make one last call on the mayor and put the problem to him as directly and as artfully as he could.

"Mr. Mayor," he planned on saying, "we need money to start a ball club." Charlie practiced this for days.

But Charlie never had to clear his throat and speak of money. Unknown to him, Mayor Low had already spoken to old and rich Hendrik Van Siclen, a long-time friend and political ally. Van Siclen knew nothing about baseball and sneered at "grown men wearing schoolboy caps and britches seeking a fortune from a horsehide ball." He was a political animal; a behind-the-scenes manipulator of men and power; a "kingmaker," so to speak. And he was the man behind Seth Low's rise to political prominence. Hendrik Van Siclen thought he saw—no doubt with the persuasive assistance and imagination of Mayor Low—a harebrain scheme to annex the Island of Manhattan to form a greater Brooklyn area—a daring act calculated to make his man, Seth Low, President of the United States.

"Not bad," he mused. "It might just work."

24

Hendrik Van Siclen was a bald, bent, senile old bachelor of ninety-one with the piercing look of a falcon. He was descended from one of the original Dutch families who first colonized the flatlands of Brooklyn—an event that occurred not long after the Indians had sold Manhattan to the Hollanders. The Van Siclens bought a piece of Brooklyn from the Canarsie Indians for a bauble or two and a bolt of cloth. It was just about the same kind of transaction the Manhattan Indians had happily concluded with Peter Minuit. In any event, the Van Siclens extended their holdings to vast tracts of land, became enormously wealthy, survived later British dominance, the War for Independence, and left their name on a number of streets, avenues, lanes, and trolley cars in the city of Brooklyn, known to them forever more as Breukelen.

Old Hendrik, still clinging to Dutch primacy in England's lost New World; old Hendrik, a sixth- or seventh-generation American, was the last in his line. There would be no more Van Siclens after him.

And there he was in the mayor's office when Charlie arrived, a beady-eyed, feisty, hawkish old man eager to bankroll the boldest reach for power his confused mind had ever encountered. Not only did he foresee the submission of Manhattan to his beloved Breukelen and Seth Low sleeping in Lincoln's bed, but also the sunlit vision of a Dutch flag once more snapping in the wind high over a restored Nieuw Netherlands. That, right there, the return of New York to Holland, the land of his forebears, would be the payment, he, Hendrik Van Siclen, would exact as the price of his support. He considered himself most fortunate to have been asked to participate in this wonderful idea.

After a few minutes of introduction and small talk about the gloomy weather—it had begun to rain—Hendrik Van Siclen was convinced that Charles Patrick O'Brien's true na-

25

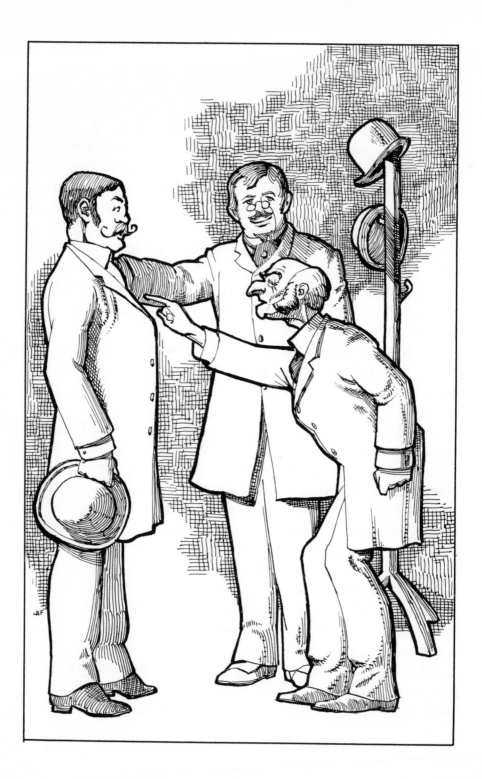

ture was devious, mysterious, and political—a Machiavellian plotter worthy of his money. He accepted the "baseball angle" as a brilliant, strategic stroke of camouflage covering a more rational goal conceived to put Seth Low in the White House. With this in his addled mind, he insisted on four conditions before he would invest a nickel of his uncountable fortune.

"My first stipulation, gentlemen, is that my involvement in this—er—a—venture be absolutely secret. Agreed?"

"Agreed."

"My second stipulation, gentlemen, is that this—er—a—venture—er—a—team, as you call it, be named the Breukelen Dutchmen. Agreed?"

"Agreed."

"Thirdly, I intend to be the sole owner and stockholder in this—er—a—club. You, Mr. O'Brien, will be campaign manager."

"You mean field manager, sir," O'Brien hastily corrected him.

"I know exactly what I mean, young man," Van Siclen snorted. "You can call it anything you wish. And don't interrupt me again."

The mayor and O'Brien glanced at each other, shrugged, and silently let the old man have his way.

"Let me add, gentlemen, that immediately upon my death, you, Mr. O'Brien, will become sole owner and stockholder."

"But, Hendrik!" the mayor protested.

"Don't but me either, Seth. I know what I am about. It would not look right for you to have any connection whatever with this thing. We want a clean operation. No skeletons in the closet. Isn't that what your administration is all about?"

"But, Hendrik!"

27

"Are we agreed, gentlemen? Or are we not?"

"Agreed."

O'Brien was pleasantly dumbfounded at what his benefactor had just offered. At ninety-one, old Hendrik did not seem long for this life. "Glory be!" Charlie muttered to himself over and over again. "Glory be!"

The mayor, slighted by his friend's largess and a bit disappointed, nevertheless saw the merit of the situation. He really did not want to be financially tied to a risky baseball business. "Let the old man and O'Brien have the headaches," he reasoned. "Brooklyn will have a team. I have nothing to lose and much to gain. I shall be remembered for having established the sport here at the very least."

"Lastly, gentlemen," Hendrik Van Siclen went on, "when the mayor becomes President . . ."

". . . of what, Hendrik?" the mayor asked with some timidity.

"Of the United States of America, of course. Now don't interrupt me again."

Seth Low coughed. O'Brien looked at him and then at Van Siclen. Charlie's robust, ruddy color had left him. His face was as gray as the weather, his eyes widening with the creeping bewilderment of a small boy. The mayor swayed momentarily but regained his composure to await Van Siclen's next surprise.

"When the mayor becomes President he will use his influence to have New York renamed Nieuw Amsterdam and so facilitate the secession of that city from the state of New York and the Union, making it possible for the House of Orange to reclaim its rightful lands in North America."

Seth Low gagged.

Hendrik Van Siclen cackled mercilessly.

The mayor's entire body began to vibrate like a plucked rubber band as he alternately coughed, gagged, and choked.

28

O'Brien pulled himself out of his own trance and gently walked the mayor to a water cooler.

"What'll we say, Mr. Mayor? Yes? No? It's the Civil War all over again. What does all this have to do with baseball? Mr. Van Siclen is mad—crazy."

Mayor Low gulped great draughts of cold water, collected himself, and rapidly reviewed their options.

"Crazy?" he whispered. "No. Just old—too old—but a might foxy. I shall never be President. However, in the event that such high office becomes my lot in life"—the mayor was not about to foreclose *that* possibility—"I shall find an honorable way out. You need not worry on either score. In the meantime, seize the opportunity as it comes. Let the future take care of itself. If we agree to this, Hendrik will supply the capital and Brooklyn will have a baseball club. My aim is to keep our fair Brooklyn independent under the terms of its Charter, the statutes of the state of New York, and within the meaning of our glorious Constitution. Your job is to give us a team that will put us on the American map. No more. No less."

"Well, gentlemen, what will it be?" Van Siclen was impatient.

"We are dealing with the devil himself," O'Brien groaned.

"We agree, Hendrik," the mayor croaked.

"Excellent! Excellent!" Van Siclen screeched. "I shall have the necessary papers drawn. We shall meet in my home on Van Siclen Avenue ten days hence for lunch— twelve noon—and sign the agreements. Agreed?"

"Agreed."

Ten days later the three men and their attorneys—all sworn to secrecy with respect to Hendrik Van Siclen's role —came together in the mansion on Van Siclen Avenue. Charles Patrick O'Brien dipped his pen into the inkwell at exactly noon and slowly signed his name to a document setting forth the old man's conditions. Mayor Low followed him with a quick illegible scrawl. Old Hendrik carefully penned his signature as did the attorneys, who acted as witnesses.

Next, Charlie O'Brien and Van Siclen repeated their signatures on another set of legal papers forming the Breukelen Dutchmen Baseball Club. Again the attorney acted as witnesses. The mayor was not included in this contract as previously agreed.

"There, gentlemen. It is done," the old man announced with glee and fell over the pile of documents stone-dead.

Without warning but not altogether unexpected, ninety-one-year-old Hendrik Van Siclen departed this world leaving Charles Patrick O'Brien sole owner and stockholder of the Breukelen Dutchmen Baseball Club before the ink had a chance to dry on the papers. Moreover, the agreement had provided Charlie with $100,000 cash now on deposit at the Van Siclen Breukelen Trust Company and access to additional funds in the amount of another $100,000 as the need arose.

Charlie O'Brien's dream had come true. He had himself a baseball club—on paper, at the moment—but nevertheless, a ball club. And the people of Brooklyn would soon know it too had a baseball team.

Mayor Seth Low led the public mourning for Hendrik Van Siclen while quietly urging Charlie to get his team together. The mayor only had eyes on the Cincinnati Red Stockings. He was anxious to make his formal challenge.

"Just hire nine players and get on with it," the mayor pleaded.

Charlie, on the other hand, was still stunned if not altogether overwhelmed by recent events. He seemed incapable of doing anything, much to the mayor's consternation. He did, however, manage to do two things following Hendrik

Van Siclen's simple funeral. He changed the spelling of Breukelen to the more familiar Brooklyn and hired Mike Noonan, owner of the Paradise Alley saloon, as assistant manager. Together they decided it would be reckless to play Cincinnati with a hastily organized team. They wanted to win. They needed time to develop a good team.

O'Brien told the mayor of their plan. Seth Low was disappointed. There was not much he could do about it. It was Charlie's club. Still, the mayor thought Charlie O'Brien owed him something. So did Charlie. O'Brien insisted on giving the mayor a few shares of stock in the club. The mayor would not hear of it. He wanted no part of the club while he was mayor. Instead, he offered a counterproposal.

"I should like to continue to demonstrate my interest, Charlie. I shall purchase some shares but only at such time as you are willing and I am no longer a public servant. Further, if in the course of my ownership of said stock I happen to be elected once more or appointed to public office, I shall divest myself of the shares giving you, my friend, the first option to buy them back. Agreed?"

"Agreed."

5.

Charlie got his team together. Finally. There it was—the Brooklyn Dutchmen, a collection of scrappy, fierce-looking, mustachioed ballplayers with poor prospects. They had a field—Dutchmen's Park—a modest field in the near geographical center of Brooklyn, the wedge-shaped corner of Utica and Remsen avenues. There were no seats for spectators. A chain kept the fans about twenty feet back from either foul line. Left field ran 283 feet back to a thick clump of bushes. Right field was just about as long but melted into a brickyard. Center field went on forever. There was nothing to define it. It was an endless meadow.

From the very first day Mayor Low made his startling announcement that Brooklyn had a baseball team, the club was in trouble. No one in organized baseball would have anything to do with them. They were an independent bunch operating outside of an established system of eight to twelve team leagues.

The Dutchmen were reduced to practicing a great deal; playing each other; playing "pickup" games with teams made up of an assortment of would-be ballplayers who assembled for the occasion; struggling against a number of other lonely independent teams like themselves; and generally pondering their uncertain future. The crowds dwindled to a sprinkling of curious people.

In desperation they sent telegrams to all the major-league teams challenging each and every one of them. The challenges were rejected. Cincinnati did not even bother to answer their telegram. Still Charlie O'Brien, Mike Noonan, and the players hung on. Some five years went by before opportunity knocked at the Dutchmen's door. It happened on Johnny Noonan's birthday. He was ten years old, skimming sea shells and growing fast.

The Staten Island Tornadoes, the worst team in the Continental League, went broke. The owners decided to get out of baseball. "Baseball has no future," they wailed. They willingly sold the club and its franchise to Charlie O'Brien for an undisclosed next-to-nothing sum. Charlie liquidated the Tornadoes, moved the franchise to the corner of Utica and Remsen avenues, and for a five-dollar fee moved the Brooklyn Dutchmen into the league place vacated by the defunct Tornadoes. The Brooklyn Dutchmen were now part of the established Continental League and ready to play in a regularly scheduled season.

From that time on until 1896—another five years—the Dutchmen batted around the league and finished last—Trenton, Dover, Schenectady, Worcester, Providence, Erie, Harrisburg, New Haven. Cincinnati still eluded them. The Red Stockings were in a different league. Yet, there was hope.

Hope, however, was a poor substitute for the lackluster attendance that plagued the Dutchmen and the rest of the league. National League competitions was becoming formidable. Competition from the other leagues did not help matters either. O'Brien had his field fenced in to give it some professional symmetry. Several rows of roofed-over seats were installed along the first- and third-base lines. That was Mike Noonan's inspiration. He seemed to think that the addition of a grandstand for the comfort of the spectators would attract more paying customers. Most of the teams in the National League had grandstands. And what was good for the rising Nationals should be good for the Dutchmen. Mike also hired private police to patrol the perimeters of the field to keep people from sneaking in without paying. None of this worked. The stands were empty for the most part. And those who sat in them had sneaked in.

Besides all this, Seth Low was no longer mayor. He was a stockholder in the club. And to make the climate even more demoralizing, his dream of a free, famous, and fabulous city of Brooklyn had become a pipe dream. The city of New York had begun a movement to annex Brooklyn and, as we now know, managed to accomplish the deed. The only thing that saved the Dutchmen from ruin was Van Siclen money.

But again opportunity knocked at the Dutchmen's door. During the closing weeks of the 1895 season, Mike Noonan talked O'Brien into hiring young Johnny as a combination bat boy, ball boy, and batting practice pitcher. His salary was eight dollars a week.

"Just lob them in, Johnny," O'Brien instructed him. "Let those big gorillas get to know what it is like to hit a ball. Nothing fancy. And remember, a baseball isn't a clam shell."

Johnny found a uniform that was too small and tight for his lanky frame. When he arrived at the pitcher's mound he looked like a corseted stick. Everyone burst out laughing. But he just stood there, tall, loose, and impassive, awaiting the first batter. He seemed to belong to the spot he was standing on.

Joe "Pirate" LaFitte, second baseman and regular lead-off man, stepped into the batter's box. "Remember, Johnny," he cautioned laughingly, "not too hard. I have a wife and five kids. They need me." Johnny did as he was told. He lobbed in the first pitch so slowly it looked like a floating cantaloupe. LaFitte did what was expected of him. He slammed the ball into center field. "Not so hard next time, Johnny," LaFitte complained. Again and again Johnny threw softly. Again and again LaFitte stroked the ball into every part of the field. He hadn't hit that well all season.

Day after day for a week, Johnny lobbed them in. Everybody hit. The young batting practice pitcher was bored. The following week he let LaFitte hit a dozen easy balls. He repeated the same performance for Joe Barlowe, the catcher, and Nate Franks, shortstop. When Binks Overstreet, the massive center fielder, came to the plate for his turn, Johnny rocked his body a couple of times and sidearmed a blazing fast ball right past him. Overstreet never saw the ball go by.

"Hey, kid, do that again," said the surprised catcher and batter in unison.

78-3734

Johnny obliged them. He whipped the ball through the strike zone. Barlowe caught it. Overstreet swung at it—in that order. Overstreet had swung too late. He missed. The pair were duly impressed.

"One more time, Johnny," O'Brien ordered. He had not seen the first pitch. He did see the second, however, and was not altogether sure of what he saw.

Johnny rocked and whipped his arm around. The blazing fast ball headed for the strike zone. This time Overstreet swung sooner, caught a piece of it, but fouled it off behind him.

"Again," O'Brien commanded as a small crowd of players gathered around him to watch the duel.

Somehow, Johnny sensed that Binks Overstreet had too much experience for him; that he would time the next pitch with precision and slam it out of the park. With the instinct that comes to natural players, Johnny "pulled the string." He rocked his body as if to throw the fast ball, came speedily around with all his strength, and lobbed one in. Ready for the fast ball, Overstreet, confused, swung mightily but too early. He missed as the ball floated to his feet and hit the ground a few inches in front of the plate.

The players laughed at Overstreet's clumsy attempt. They did not laugh at Johnny Noonan. Johnny was the miracle they had been waiting for. With more seasoning and careful handling, Johnny Noonan and his arm would put the Dutchmen at the top of their league. And if he was as good as he seemed to be, the Continental League itself might amount to something.

The word went out. The Dutchmen had the greatest young pitcher in all of baseball. Johnny remained a bat boy, ball boy, and batting practice pitcher during the final weeks of the schedule. But people began to come out to the park and paid the price of admission just to see Johnny pitch batting practice.

Professionals came to watch Johnny also. Scouts, coaches, and managers of other teams. More astonishingly, representatives of teams from other leagues came to see what all the fuss was about. They liked what they saw.

"When are you going to play him, O'Brien?" they all wanted to know.

"I have no idea," said O'Brien. "It's too late for this season. The boy is young. He's only fourteen years old. Johnny's got plenty of time."

"What about next year? Will he be ready?"

"That depends." O'Brien was being cagey.

"On what?"

"On what he shows us over the winter and next spring." O'Brien was already planning to rent space in an armory over the winter so that Johnny could practice.

"Will you let him play some exhibition games next spring?"

"We might."

By the time the 1895 season had ended, the Brooklyn Dutchmen Baseball Club had received firm offers from all twelve of the National League clubs to play exhibition games during the spring of 1896.

"We are on the map," Seth Low proclaimed to one and all. "Brooklyn is on the map!"

By mid-November, Charlie O'Brien and his assistant manager, Mike Noonan, had decided to accept only two of the invitations. It would be foolhardy, they reasoned, to take on the whole National League. Besides, their own schedule would not permit it. They chose Baltimore, the best team in the league—just to see how well they could do against them —and the Cincinnati club, a mediocre team that had long been on Seth Low's and Charlie O'Brien's list of things to do. They had a chance, they figured, against Cincinnati. Baltimore could clobber them. But then again with strong pitching—meaning Johnny Noonan, and he was improving every day in the armory—they might just pull it off.

Both the Baltimore club and the Cincinnati club said they would play the Dutchmen as home games, that is, in Baltimore and in Cincinnati. Also, they offered to pay all travel expenses for the Dutchmen or guarantee them a substantial sum of money for their day's work. The Dutchmen turned down the expense money offer but accepted the guaranteed fee. The entire deal was contingent on the Dutchmen's guarantee that Johnny Noonan would be the starting pitcher for both games. If, for some reason, Johnny could not pitch, then the game would go on, but the guaranteed fee would be canceled. O'Brien gleefully agreed to everything and promised to deliver Johnny Noonan.

He did. And Johnny Noonan was whacked in the head by a foul ball in Baltimore.

The Cincinnati game was three weeks off.

II.

Time is a walk down the hall
    or walking tall.
Time was back then
    or will be when.
Time is the umpire's call:
    "Play ball!"

1.

Johnny Noonan lay on his bed in the dreary accident ward of the Johns Hopkins Hospital, unmoving, alive, out of touch with time and place. A draped partition hid him from several of the groaning occupants of the other eleven beds that filled the narrow room. Mike Noonan sat on a stool oblivious to the continuous march of a starchy nurse applying cold compresses to his son's unfortunate head. A doctor came. He listened to Johnny's heart, took his pulse, lifted his eyelids to study his vacant eyes, rested one hand softly on Mike's shoulder, shrugged, and left. Mike stared at the still form of his son and said nothing.

Once Mike thought he noticed Johnny's eyes twitch as if he were trying to open them. He thought he saw his mouth move with the effort.

"You're imagining things," the nurse assured him. "I did not notice any movement. Why don't you wait in the visitors' room, Mr. Noonan? We'll call you if there is a change in your son's condition."

Mike refused to budge from his stool.

Charlie O'Brien came to the ward dragging a remorseful Jack Eastman with him. He shoved Big Jack through the partition to take a good look at what he had done by swinging late at a bad ball.

"If I'da known, Mr. Noonan. If only I'da known," was all Eastman could muster before he fled.

"How's the boy doing, Mike?" O'Brien cautiously asked once Big Jack Eastman had scrambled out of the ward.

"I don't know, Charlie. He's so still."

"Don't worry, Mike. He'll be all right. Wait and see."

"That's exactly what I'm doing. Waiting and seeing. Nothing is happening. By the way, how did the team do?"

"We lost twelve–three, officially. But the way I look at it we won, unofficially. We had them three–nothing until Johnny got rapped on the noggin. Eastman! That overstuffed gorilla! I'd like to plant him in one of these beds right here in this ward! Johnny will be healthy for Cincinnati, though. Mark my word!" O'Brien was not all that convinced as he glanced at the pale young pitcher flat on his back, his head packed in cold compresses. He was telling himself not to worry.

"Sure, Charlie. Sure," Mike listlessly whispered.

"Gentlemen! Please!" the nurse scolded. "You will both simply have to leave. This patient needs absolute quiet."

"She's right, Mike. What do you say? How 'bout some coffee?"

Mike stirred from the stool to which he had been rooted and permitted Charlie O'Brien to lead him slowly out of the ward. The nurse followed them out.

None of them heard Johnny groan and mumble. Nor did they see him jerk his head from side to side as if he were being slapped by some great invisible hand. Finally, he quit moving and said quite plainly, "Hey. Cut it out, Wires. I'm okay."

None of them heard that either!

42

2.

"Hey. Cut it out, Wires. I'm okay."

That was all Johnny Noonan said before he became limply quiet again. He seemed to be talking to no one present—certainly no one in the immediate vicinity of his bed. No one was there. And no one answered to the name of "Wires." His mouth moved, forming words that surfaced from somewhere deep inside his subconscious. Yet his eyes remained shut, his body numb, unseeing and unfeeling of the hospital environment in which he now existed. Every so often his entire face would twitch as if to rid itself of a pesky mosquito bent on disturbing an interesting dream. By every symptom, description, and examination, Johnny Noonan was medically unconscious, struck down by a foul ball. He never knew what hit him. Nevertheless, a distantly vague and floating part of him seemed to be awake, unhooked, as it were, from the rest of his immobile body and brain.

The foul ball that had laid Johnny Noonan low had somehow short-circuited an unknown physiological connection and pushed him to the far edge of another time and place. Whatever and wherever that part of him was, it was responding to a mysterious stimulus buried far inside his own mystifying self. Not even Johnny Noonan, however unconscious he was at the moment, was subconsciously aware of the jolting transformation that had sent him rushing into the year 1996—one hundred years beyond where he was.

43

Big Jack Eastman's foul ball did indeed knock Johnny Noonan into the next century!

The man slapped Johnny Noonan a few times to bring him around. Johnny did not seem seriously hurt. A box of baseballs had fallen from the warehouse shelf and hit the rangy, big-handed youth on the head. He was momentarily stunned.

"Okay, Johnny. Snap out of it. That's the boy. You are going to be just fine. You're pitching tomorrow, you know. We can't have our ace starter on the disabled list."

Johnny shook his head to clear his mental fog and squinted at Vince "Wires" Marconi, the muscular man who had been slapping him. "I'm all right, Wires, I guess," Johnny replied, feeling his head for any bumps or bruises. There were none.

"Okay, kid. Good enough. No harm done. Whew! You gave me a scare. Tell you what. Why don't you go home and relax. The store closes in an hour anyway. And I want you a winner tomorrow."

Vincent Marconi, ex-ballplayer—he picked up the nickname "Wires" as a rookie, an obvious reference to the great Marconi, inventor of wireless radio—was the owner of Marconi's Sport Mart, a Brooklyn discount sporting goods store. He was genuinely concerned about his fifteen-year-old stockclerk right-hander, Johnny Noonan. Johnny threw for the Spartans, a team in the teen-age local Hank Aaron League. Wires was the team's sponsor and enjoyed seeing his name "Marconi's Sport Mart" emblazoned on the backs of the

club uniforms. But more than that, Wires Marconi was a scout for his former team, the New York Mets, and Johnny Noonan was a very young hot prospect that deserved his fullest attention and devotion.

"Stick with me, kid," Wires constantly told Johnny, "and you'll wind up in the National League."

In the year 1996, the National League was the only major baseball league. Its chief rival, the American League, had vanished after almost ninety years of competition. Among themselves, the American League teams played first-rate baseball. It spawned some of the greatest athletes ever to play the game—Ruth, Gehrig, Hornsby, DiMaggio, Lajoie, Waddell, Cobb, Speaker, Frank Robinson, Bert Campaneris, Jimmie Foxx, and more. But in fifteen years—not since before 1981—the American League was unable to beat the National League either in an All-Star game or in the World Series. The losses themselves were not the real problem. The demise of the American League was hastened by a calamitous event that shook the world in 1983 and made baseball only one of its victims.

The world ran out of oil.

The American League, having no seniority over the National League, was abandoned in a move to conserve energy.

Mike Noonan and Charlie O'Brien returned to the partition that shielded the unconscious Johnny Noonan from the rest of the ward. Johnny seemed to be breathing easier. Some color had returned to his face. The cold compresses were gone. But peaceful, comatose Johnny was elsewhere—walking home on a Brooklyn street one hundred years beyond the partition that surrounded his bed—beyond the accident ward of Johns Hopkins Hospital in Baltimore. Unbeknowing to his father, his manager, and all of science, Johnny Noonan had become his own grandson. The future had revealed itself. Its messenger was a foul baseball.

Baseball in 1996 had changed more severely during the preceding sixteen years than it had changed in one hundred and fifty years of competition. It was not the same game Vincent "Wires" Marconi played when he caught for the New York Mets back in 1983. That was his last year in the big leagues. For a while most people imagined 1983 to be the last year of civilization, perhaps of the planet earth as well. Within one searing week that taxes the imagination—the first week following the October rite of the World Series—Cincinnati took four straight from the star-strewn Yankees—civilization had stopped working for want of oil. While the industrial nations of the world froze in fright, the baseball moguls met in warm Key West, Florida, and voted to keep the national pastime alive no matter what the cost.

"The very morale of this great nation," said the commissioner in a televised interview, "is at stake. We intend to adapt to the situation with every means at our disposal. Professional baseball lives," he shouted, "and will live on!"

The shocking, terrifying events of that one October week in 1983 will be remembered through eternity. And for too many of the ordinary people of the civilized world, eternity came and went during that week.

The calamity began in far-off Iran, heretofore an oil-rich country bordering on the Soviet Union. Iranian wells, which had been producing millions of barrels of crude oil a day for years, suddenly, and without warning, slowed down to a mere trickle. The Russians, suspecting an international plot to bring them to their knees, demanded and received permission to inspect the Iranian oil fields. The Russian inspection tour never got under way. Their own fields in the Ukraine had run dry. Within hours every major oil field in the world had reported they were bone dry—Ploeşti in Romania; Saudi Arabia; Kuwait; Libya; Iraq; Venezuela; Mexico; Texas, Oklahoma, Pennsylvania, offshore California, and Louisiana in the United States; and vast fields in southwestern China, the existence of which had been, until then, a well-guarded secret.

"It was as if a cosmic syringe had been inserted into the earth's crust," the New York *Times* editorialized, "and drew forth every ounce of black gold that had been on deposit beneath for a million years."

On a lesser scale, on more human terms, the disaster was not much different from inserting a needle in someone's vein and drawing off every ounce of life-giving blood.

The crisis was turned over to the United Nations for a speedy solution. There, all the distinguished scientists of the world gathered and waited for the member nations to agree on an agenda to deal with the calamity. They debated for three days and finally announced that "in view of the fact that current world-wide reserves of crude and refined oil will be depleted in six months, we have unanimously agreed to pass the problem on to the United Nations Educational, Scientific, and Cultural Organization. UNESCO will open formal discussion in Paris on the first day of next month."

Press reaction was instantaneous.

"Doomsday," screamed the San Francisco *Chronicle,* still smarting from a series of tremors that knocked a few buildings off their foundations the day before the world ran out of oil.

"Buck passers," bellowed the New York *Post.* Inside, in the sports section, was a picture of Vince "Wires" Marconi receiving a new Cadillac from Mets fans honoring his retirement from baseball.

The St. Louis *Post-Dispatch* philosophized about the "warm-blooded human race" and cautioned everyone to "bundle up for the long winter ahead."

The Philadelphia *Inquirer* ran a banner headline announcing, "Neo Ice Age Imminent."

The man on the street took things a trifle less hysterically, trusting in the inevitable victory of science over nature, and blaming politicians for the whole nasty business. Northerners, who took no chances, packed their belongings and fled south, leaving their oil burners, overshoes, snow tires, and antifreeze to roving looters. Cold weather enthusiasts headed north to hole up in primitive cabins, trusting in the unending supply of firewood to heat their lives. People with no place to go occasionally wandered out to buy black-market petroleum products or join an angry mob or two to demolish any number of local gas stations. Pickets appeared in front of such places as the Mobil Building on New York City's Forty-second Street, protesting Mobil Oil's complicity in the destruction of the ecology. Exxon, Sohio, and Gulf, among others, also came in for their share of pickets. By and large, things seemed under control. No one declared martial law. The fact of the matter was that the news was just too mind-boggling to accept. It was positively unreal— not to be believed.

The world, precariously balanced on the edge of a fright-

ful abyss—if it was not already slipping toward doomsday, a witness to its own self-destruction with the disappearance of oil, its most valuable natural resource—was strangely quiet.

During the next six years, between 1983 and 1989, scientists everywhere worked frantically to bring to the fearful world new sources and systems of energy. At the same time, governments struggled to maintain an image of confidence in the face of altering life styles and drastically reduced work and leisure-time activities.

"The solution is within reach," the public was continuously reminded. But there was little evidence of this to impress the public.

America had turned to coal as an interim solution. Within weeks the entire country was covered with a gloomy blanket of soot. Soon coal—and there was plenty of it—was rationed lest it, too, mysteriously disappear. Americans struggled to hold onto their time-honored optimism while waiting for a miracle. Had it not been for around-the-clock TV movies, variety shows, sports, and soap operas—a schedule that eliminated all talk shows and regular news—there were periodic cheerful progress reports on the crisis—the fabric of American life would have unraveled.

By 1990, however, the miracle began to work. The trials of the harrowing eighties began to subside, dissipated, so to speak, by the success of crash programs that provided widespread use of atomic power, solar energy, and improved agricultural fertilizers. A new world was at hand. Everyone sensed it. An oil-less world, sweet and reliable, bright with eternal promise. And with that eternal promise came the familiar sniping of the great powers, each of whom claimed credit for the soon-to-be paradise.

"We did it!" cried all America. "Yankee ingenuity."

"Soviet science is the true victor!" replied *Pravda.*

"Oriental patience," cooed the New China News Agency.

Saudi Arabia, Iraq, Kuwait, and Libya said nothing. Iran kept her sullen silence, too, and renamed herself Persia as a reminder of her ancient, glorious past.

Professional baseball staggered through the crises and survived. The game bent with the times. It had to. The fans could not get out to the ball parks unless they walked. Few of them tried. Unable to support the fading business of their clubs, the owners, each and every one of them, sold out to a conglomeration of partnerships of the TV networks and advertising agencies. The new owners immediately liquidated the American League in the interest of consolidation, conservation, and smart business. Three American League teams were saved, however, for sentimental reasons: the New York Yankees, the Cleveland Indians, and the Detroit Tigers. These clubs were incorporated in an expanded National League whose Eastern and Western Divisions would henceforth produce their own pennant winners to face one another in a single-league World Series.

Now the national pastime had a new beat and a new direction. It was aimed at the pay-as-you-watch home TV viewer. Although the world was rescuing itself from the awful crisis of the 1980s, by 1990 it was too late to return the game of baseball to the ball park fans. There simply were no longer any ball parks as such. Great complexes like Shea and Yankee stadiums or Candlestick Park were reduced to field houses. They were stripped of their seats, walled in, and roofed over. Every ball park in the major league had, in effect, become a TV studio. There was one exception, however, Chicago's Wrigley Field, home of the Chicago Cubs. True to the tradition and feistiness of the Wrigley family, who bought back their club from NBC–J. Walter Thompson, Inc., Wrigley Field continued to resist modernization. They turned their backs years ago on artificial turf, night games, and all-weather roofing, and they intended to keep it that way as long as Americans chewed gum. They refused to remove the old seats as well. The whole place creaked worse than ever. And the Cubs had not had a winner in forty-five years. Not since 1945.

Wrigley Field continued to be filled with cheering crowds for every home game—a phenomenon in the eyes of the country; absolute defiance in the eyes of the Commissioner of Baseball. The new owners brought a suit against the Cubs to make them conform to the rules. But the Wrigleys had their field declared a National Monument by an act of Congress and the suit was thrown out of court. After that, the Cubs management would not allow a television camera within fifteen miles of the place—a house policy that was unofficially enforced by the Chicago Police Department. Secretly, there was not a ballplayer anywhere that did not want to play in Wrigley Field. The roar of the crowds was marvelous, almost symphonic, not to mention the fresh air.

"That's baseball," the old-timers crooned. The players loved it.

7.

The doctors at Johns Hopkins Hospital were becoming increasingly mystified. Johnny Noonan's vital signs—pulse, heart, respiration, and reflexes—were all normal. His leg jumped when they tapped his knee. His toes wiggled when they scraped the soles of his feet. Yet, he remained in a deep slumber unable to hear the pleas for him to awaken.

"We are confronted with a most unusual case," one doctor intoned. "The patient is not responding and he should be. He appears to be well. Look at him. He is perfectly content wherever he is."

By 1996 the United States was well on its way toward recovery. Coal as a heating fuel was being used less and less, replaced in small homes by solar energy and in large buildings by central atomic power plants. Traffic congestion, too, was becoming its old familiar self to those people who had lived through the crisis and were old enough to remember the "good old days." Those few private and public vehicles that had converted to charcoal burning as a fuel had all but disappeared, replaced by humming electric cars and buses. The years-old layer of soot had nearly vanished. The country was beginning to sparkle again.

Also, by 1996, every major-league ballstudio—once called "ball park" or "ball field"—was electronically engineered—all, that is, save Wrigley Field. Some of the minor-league parks—Tidewater being an outstanding example—were as electronically complete as the major-league ballstudios. The rest, along with the thousands of other sand-lot, Little League, PAL, American Legion, and Hank Aaron League fields, were what they had always been—outdoor dirt-grass fields.

Perhaps the most startling change of all was the absence of umpires. The youngsters born during the crisis or a year or two before never thrilled to the call "Play ball." TV directors began each game by pointing to the pitcher off camera. Scanning devices and other sensitive electronic gear determined the outcome of every play. Home plate glowed green or red beneath an electronic strike zone—green for a ball, red for a strike or foul. If a pitcher interrupted his motion, or balked, that too was picked up by an electronic device that set off a bell at the pitcher's mound. All of these signals, or impulses, and more were fed into a central computer located directly behind home plate—some fifteen feet behind the catcher—protected by impenetrable, shatterproof glass. The computer stored the records and statistics of the game and made all final decisions while registering the game's progress on the center-field scoreboard as always. The computer was also connected to "status panels" located in the team dugouts so that the managers would have an immediate and handy reference to work out strategy. The whole playing field operated like a gigantic pinball machine.

All this was under the direct supervision of one man, the technical umpire—tech-ump for short. The home viewer shortened this even further to the more popular "chump." The chump sat at his own computer console, which included an instant replay device, high above and behind home plate and out of sight. A few traditional umpires were kept on "standby alert" in the event the computer and its scanning devices broke down, an event that happened on occasion.

Another radical change in the game was the elimination of public instant replay. The new owners—the networks and advertising agencies—felt that this was a waste of good commercial spots. Now, in addition to the regular commercials between innings, and before and after each game, there are ten-second commercials after each play.

55

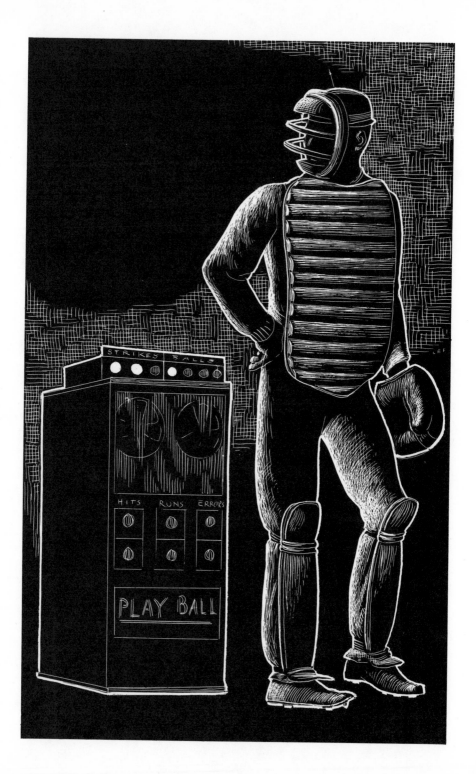

With it all, no one doubted for a minute that the heroes of baseball were still the players. The clutch hitters, the acrobatic shortstops, fearless third basemen, fast-ball pitchers, and gazellelike center fielders—this was the stuff that made the game. But here, too, nothing was as it was the day before the world ran out of oil. Now the players came from everywhere around the globe—the United States, Latin America, the Caribbean Islands, Russia, Japan, China, India, Italy, France, Indonesia, Ceylon, England, Australia, and Iceland. The once oil-rich countries of the Middle East were excluded by mutual consent of the owners. They tried to keep the Russians and Chinese out also, but failed to do so, bowing to strong pressure from the Congress and President. The Israelis, on the other hand, refused to allow any of their citizens to play American baseball as a good will gesture to the Arabs. It seemed to work. There was talk now of Middle East solidarity and that the Arabs and Israelis would soon end more than a generation of bickering.

The international aspect of the American National Pastime caused the federal government to create the Office of Sport, within the State Department, appointing the Commissioner of Baseball to the concurrent post of Undersecretary of Sport. At the same time, the government saw to it that a number of undercover agents were sprinkled among the various teams as players to keep tabs on the foreign athletes in the event that some of them were espionage plants—spies.

By 1996 every player was equipped with a microscopic transistor receiver to keep him in touch with the dugout. Obviously, there was no further need for hand signals from the third-base coach to the batter. The transistors created a whole new aspect to the game. Each club had to employ linguists to reach their non-English-speaking players. Often a game came to an interminable standstill as simultaneous translations were being made to the players. Usually when this happened—and it happened very often—the home-viewing audiences were subjected to a flood of commercials that destroyed the rhythm of the game and brought on a flood of complaining phone calls.

For a while all the clubs developed techniques for jamming the tiny receivers with a variety of noises to prevent a player from receiving instructions or to rattle him so much he committed errors. This was against the rules. The penalty, if caught, was a huge fine. One manager, who was also an undercover agent, secretly employed other agents to intercept opposition signals, decode them, if necessary, and refeed false information to the players involved on their own team's frequency. When the other owners found out about his activities, the manager was thrown out of baseball. No one ever knew or suspected that he was an undercover agent working all the time for the State Department.

One of the more distracting innovations of the 1990s was the system used for ballplayer identification. They still retained the traditional numeral and name across the backs of their uniforms—which, incidentally, was a one-piece zippered jump suit. But underneath these, across the lower back of the uniform, was a nine-bar metallic figure—a series of shiny stripes of various thicknesses—that identified the player for the electronic scanners and other devices which programmed the computer. The back of the uniform looked like a supermarket box of breakfast cereal.

Baseball had bent with the times.

9.

The nurse studied the chart at the foot of Johnny Noonan's iron bed. She clucked with sympathy at the unconscious boy before her. The chart indicated that Johnny had been brought to the hospital at 2:10 P.M., Friday, April 3, 1896; that he had been treated; periodically examined; and showed no apparent signs of imminent recovery. The reason for his admittance was recorded as "head blow, parietal, left, no fracture, unconscious."

The nurse took his pulse once more. It was perfectly normal. She noted this on the chart, scribbled in the time and date—5:40 P.M., Friday, April 3, 1896—and added the comment, "still comatose."

The future went on revealing itself.

10.

By the middle of the 1990s, everyone—mostly Americans—had soured. Life had become a humming bore. The whole country was enveloped in the monotonous drone of automation. The dreary drone of machinery powered by atoms or the sun—machinery that invaded everyone's existence and ran everything—was altogether too pleasant sounding, intoxicating. It produced a numbing, sleep-inducing effect that exhausted the country's great creative instincts. People would rather watch television and sleep than do anything else.

The hard fact was that by the middle 1990s, Americans had stopped making whatever it was they used to make—cars, TV sets, home appliances, clothes, books, paintings, bats, balls, gloves—everything. Americans imported what they needed and did not need. They used them, serviced them, advertised them, sold them secondhand, or threw them away. Americans created nothing—not even the computers that ran baseball, or the countless machines that hummed without letup—nothing. And baseball, the national pastime, became the tedious symbol of the new malaise.

The trouble was that people no longer had a clear idea what they were supposed to be or do. Once in a while a baseball manager, furious with frustration, would kick dirt at the computer behind home plate—or rather at its impenetrable, shatter-proof protective glass. The terrorizing wail of a screaming siren would rise from the core of the computer. The manager would be immediately ejected from the field by TV studio police. The stay-at-home fans enjoyed these "rhubarbs" and demanded more.

Yet, with it all, they were beginning to lose interest in the national pastime. With a baseball crisis in the offing, the New York Mets decided to revive Old-timers' Day at Shea Ballstudio. It was the first Old-timers' Day in twenty years. Joe DiMaggio was there in his old Number Five Yankee uniform looking tan and fit. He would not see eighty-five again. Tom Seaver still looked boyish despite his baldness and girth. He weighed about 275 pounds and was a United States senator from California. Nolan Ryan, whose lifetime pitching record included seventeen no-hitters, could only throw underhand. Pete Rose, the onetime *enfant terrible* of the Cincinnati Reds, was there, too. He was now manager of the Yankees. Rose took his turn at bat and slammed one

of Ryan's underhand change-ups into the electronic scanner near third base setting it on fire and knocking out the central computer behind the plate. Johnny Bench, Rose's former teammate, squatting in the on-deck circle, his aging hulk seeming to occupy the entire space, watched calmly as the sparks flew. A broad grin covered his ample face.

The game was held up for about forty minutes until the fires were extinguished and the old-time umpires came back on the field. The old-timers' game went on a few more innings while the TV home audience turned their quiet fascination into noisy delirium. The fans—millions of them—liked what they saw. They called, wired, and wrote the commissioner demanding reruns of old-time games of the sixties and seventies. They refused to pay for any more of the kind of studio baseball they had been given. They wanted to see real crowds, real umps, rhubarbs, excitement—humanity. Thousands of them descended on Wrigley Field in Chicago to see the action live and as it used to be. Wrigley Field could not handle them all. Fighting broke out. Troops and police rushed to the scene. The rioting went on for three days in June 1996 before it ran out of steam. It was the worst, the meanest, public demonstration of any kind ever witnessed in the United States.

"How do you feel, kid?" Wires Marconi asked his protégé, Johnny Noonan. "Any aftereffects?"

"No," Johnny answered, touching his head gingerly in a number of places. Johnny rubbed the back of his skull on the left side—the parietal bone of the cranium—where the falling box of baseballs had nicked him. He felt nothing.

"Good!" Wires declared. "Let's get to it."

Wires Marconi and Johnny arrived at the Prospect Park diamond where the Spartans were scheduled to play the Red Hook Sabers. They arrived long before anyone else. Wires always did that—arrive early. He liked to warm up Johnny himself. Wires knew a great deal about pitching and pitchers. During his playing days he was considered the best handler of young pitchers around. Now he had Johnny Noonan, who he knew would someday pitch in the National League and become a great star. Wires was not about to permit anyone else to handle young Johnny Noonan.

Johnny did a couple of loosening-up exercises—knee bends, stretches, and whatnot—and then ran a few short circles.

"What did you think of those riots, Wires?" the young pitcher asked as he wiped his face with a towel.

"Don't think about them, kid. Just throw the ball." Wires had already positioned himself behind home plate and was smashing his huge fist into the pocket of the mitt. It felt good. He felt good to be where he was—behind home plate. Wires was ready.

Johnny was ready, too. He picked up a ball and twirled it around in his hand. He looked up at the warm morning sky and took a deep breath. He felt good. He put his foot on the rubber, rocked back and forth, and threw the first ball in easily.

"Atta boy, Johnny. Throw a few more like that, then put a little head on it."

Johnny threw four or five more warm-ups.

"You're looking good, kid. Now show me a half speed down the pike."

Johnny rocked and threw. The ball came straight in, but

as it reached the front edge of the plate, it suddenly dipped and curved away from Marconi's glove.

"Hey! I didn't call for that. Now throw it half speed straight. And don't overhand it like you just did. Where did you pick that up? Show me your sidearm."

Johnny showed Wires the sidearm. The ball came in straight and on target. Nothing fancy.

"That's more like it, kid. Now show me a three-quarter speed curve."

The ball came in with good speed and gently swerved away. The overhand curve that Johnny had thrown minutes before had more on it than this faster pitch. Wires knew that immediately.

"Let me see that overhand again, kid. Put something on it."

Johnny flipped the ball in his hand until it felt right, concentrated on the pitch for a second or two, drew a deep breath, rocked back and forth, and fired the ball in. It came at Wires as if it were shot out of a cannon. For a split moment, Wires did not know whether to stand his ground and catch it or get out of the way.

And then it happened! As before, the pitch was right down the middle heading for a perfect strike. But unlike before, as the ball reached the plate's front edge, it did not dip and curve away. It took a sharp right-angle turnaway from Wires and landed about ninety feet away on the first-base side of the diamond.

Wires and Johnny looked with disbelief at the ball resting on a tuft of weeds.

"What was that?" the astounded Marconi asked, still not taking his eyes off the ball. "What did you do?"

"I didn't do anything, Wires. I just threw it."

"Come on now, kid. That ball doesn't have an atomic engine inside. Give."

64

"Honest, Wires. I didn't do anything. All I did was concentrate on the pitch, leaned on it, and . . ."

"And what?"

"And hoped it would do what it did—turn a corner."

"Nobody can do that! Nobody! It must have been something in the air. Maybe the ball is magnetized or something like that. Throw me another one. Only this time use another ball—sidearm."

Johnny took another ball and went into his motion. He whipped the ball in from the side, his arm seeming to crack like a whip. The ball appeared to come screaming in from left field. As it reached the front edge of home plate it came to a dead stop and hung in the air. Wires lunged for it. The ball dropped harmlessly to the ground. Wires fell clumsily over it.

"I don't believe it! It's impossible to do that! And don't tell me you hoped it would do that!"

"I did, Wires. So help me!"

"One more time, kid. Use another ball."

Again Johnny whipped the ball in. Again it stopped dead in front of home plate. Wires stared at the suspended ball. Suddenly the ball shot ahead as Wires made a grab for it. It slammed into his mitt.

"Listen, kid. I don't know what's going on. But until I find out that you really have something no one else has; that you can monkey with a baseball like no one else can, you are not pitching today."

The next day, Sunday, Wires took Johnny to an empty distant lot. There was not a soul around for miles. Wires made sure of that.

"Okay, kid," he began. "Do it again."

Johnny did not oblige Marconi immediately. He took his time warming up. "Are you ready, Wires? This one's going over your head."

"Just throw a strike, kid. Do your stuff. But throw strikes."

Johnny flung the fast ball straight at Marconi. Marconi got set to catch it, figuring that Johnny was kidding about sending the ball over his head. However, just as the ball was about to reach Marconi's mitt in the strike zone it abruptly changed course. It rose vertically about six feet without losing its velocity, turned the corner, and went zipping over Marconi's head.

The amazed Marconi began calling for one weird pitch after the other. The equally amazed Johnny threw them. At one point, Johnny dropped Marconi's return throw. It rolled a few feet away. Johnny looked at the ball intently. It rolled back to where he stood. Johnny never moved except to pick it up.

"Okay, kid, that's it," Wires announced. "You're through with the Spartans. No more Hank Aaron League baseball for you. We're heading for the Mets and the big time."

"You mean it, Wires?"

"I wouldn't say it if I didn't mean it, would I? But first there are a couple of things we've got to get straight. Then you and I are going to pay a visit to a friend of mine—a shrink—you know, a psychologist. In the meantime, I'm going to speak to the Mets front office. Eddie Kranepool, their player development chief, is a good friend of mine. I'm going to see if we can't arrange a tryout."

"Great, Wires. But what's there to straighten out?"

"I want the truth, kid. Didn't you once tell me that you had a grandfather who played pro ball? And that he threw some kind of screwball that no one else could throw?"

"That's right."

"What was his name?"

"Johnny Noonan."

"Same as yours?"

66

"Yes."

"Never heard of him. But that's neither here nor there. Did he ever teach you how to throw?"

"No. He couldn't. He died before I was born."

"Okay. That takes care of that. But how come you never showed me this new stuff of yours before yesterday."

"Beats me, Wires. I didn't know I had stuff like that. It's funny though."

"What's funny?"

"Well, after that box of baseballs hit me in the head, right here"—Johnny pointed to the back of his head—"my eyes felt strange. Cold. I could make things get large or small like a camera lens. It was like I was a human zoom lens. When I got home on Friday, I practiced doing that in my room until it suddenly went away. I didn't wish anything to change direction until yesterday. And you've got to believe me, Wires, when I wished that ball to turn the corner yesterday, I was only daydreaming."

"That's what you think, kid. We are going to see my friend, the doctor, tonight."

Jim Franzheim was a highly touted psychologist who spent most of his time in research shedding new light on human behavior. The profusion of diplomas, certificates, framed pictures and letters on his office wall gave silent testimony to his far-reaching recognition. He was visiting psychologist at Brooklyn's Maimonides Hospital; professor emeritus of psychology at both Brooklyn College and the Downstate

Medical School; and former president of the American Association of Psychologists. Jim Franzheim had credentials. Now, well along in years and an incurable fan of old-time baseball—he owned a collection of more than five hundred bubblegum baseball cards—he was, in his retirement, team psychologist for the New York Mets.

It was not his usual practice to see patients at midnight. In fact he was usually in bed by 9 P.M. sharp. But when Wires called him and asked for the unusual appointment in the interest of the Mets and "national security," he quickly agreed.

When Marconi and Johnny were ushered into Dr. Franzheim's office, Wires immediately pledged him to the utmost secrecy. He then introduced him to Johnny Noonan and excitedly described Johnny's pitching prowess. Dr. Franzheim was very attentive and expressionless. For a moment the thought crossed his mind that Vincent "Wires" Marconi was the one who needed help. These were very trying times. Even the most rational and level-headed members of the community go off the deep end nowadays. Perhaps, on second thought, Marconi had indeed come up with some kind of phenomenon. Why not? Crazier things than this have happened in recent history. The world ran dry, didn't it? Nothing would surprise him any more.

"We shall see what we shall see," the doctor gravely intoned when Wires finished his summary.

"Look, Doc. Johnny here has got potential. Even without his screwballs he is destined for a major-league spot. But this thing is different—stupendous. And I've got to have some answers before the Mets take a look at him."

"We shall see what we shall see," Dr. Franzheim repeated. "I shall give the subject a few simple tests and we'll take it from there."

He produced a ball from his desk drawer, cleared a table

nearby, and placed the ball in the center of the table.

"All right, young man. Let me see you move the ball without touching it or breathing on it."

He positioned Johnny about seven or eight feet from the table and stepped aside. He motioned to Wires to stand beside him. Johnny spent a minute concentrating on the ball. He was nervous and perspiring. He was not sure he could do as he was asked. He was a pitcher, not a magician. Presently, the ball started to move toward one corner of the table, slowly. It then proceeded to travel more deliberately around the four edges of the table coming to rest at the center.

Wires poked the flabbergasted doctor, "See. What did I tell you? What's the story, Doc?"

"I'm not sure I saw what I saw," said the psychologist, trying to collect himself. "Do something else, young man."

Johnny fixed his gaze on the ball once more. The ball rose from the table and traveled clear across the room, where it softly landed on the doctor's desk. For the next hour Johnny moved the ball, a paperweight, and a variety of other small objects from one place to another in a number of directional ways.

"Well, Doc, what is it?"

"In my opinion—I would have to study this phenomenon more closely, you realize—in my opinion this young man is a psychokinetic."

"A what?"

"Just as I said. A psychokinetic. I have heard of such a phenomenon but I never thought it was possible. I must write a paper on this."

"Not yet, Doc. Remember, this has got to remain a secret for the time being. We'll tell you when you can write a paper. First explain what the disease is."

"It's not a disease, Wires. Kinetics, first of all, is a science that has to do with the motion of masses in relation to other forces acting on them. It's very complicated. I am not sure I understand it myself. A psychokinetic, however, is someone who can exert certain forces upon objects. That is to say, this someone can transmit peculiar energy to objects and actually direct their movements without laying a hand on them. In the case of a pitcher, he can—if he is a psychokinetic— he can throw the ball and change its course or direction in mid-flight. In other words, he can make the ball do whatever he wants it to do regardless of what the batter does. Obviously, if a psychokinetic pitcher meets up with a psychokinetic batter, you've got the classic immovable object meeting the irresistible force—zap—nothing—checkmate. My God, Wires, the ramifications of this are awesome."

"Thanks, Doc. Thanks for everything. Send your bill to the Mets. They are going to love Johnny Noonan."

"Pitch, young feller," said the Mets aging pitching coach, Jerry Koosman.

Johnny stepped to the mound to face Ramón Bimmelstern, a veteran slugger from Argentina. Johnny surveyed the small cluster of people representing the Mets management—Koosman; Kranepool; Willie Stargell, former Pittsburgh Pirate great and now Met batting coach; Imogene Gibson, a Ph.D. in Slavic languages from Howard University, a utility infielder, and the first playing-manager of her sex; and J. Phelps Wiggington, recent past vice-president of ABC's Department of Public Affairs and now Met president.

Johnny glanced at Wires. Wires leaned against the tarpaulin that screened the tryout from the unauthorized curious—Wires had insisted on that—and nodded his silent encouragement.

Johnny stared at the batter and catcher, inhaled deeply, rocked, and unleashed a sidearm sizzler that headed straight for the strike zone. The batter took a vicious cut at nothing. The ball never got there. Johnny reversed its course. The ball landed back in his own glove.

Wires smiled an all-knowing smile. The Mets brass was stunned.

"Give me that ball," Koosman demanded. "What have you got on it? A rubber band?"

The brass examined the ball. It was clean and new.

"Give him another ball," Manager Gibson ordered. "One more time, son," she added.

Johnny whipped in another sure strike. This time the ball stopped inches in front of the plate. Bimmelstern stared at the suspended ball hypnotically, disbelieving. The Mets management was stupefied. It was so quiet, so still, that if it was not for the steady low humming of civilization, one could have heard the proverbial pin drop.

Stargell broke the silence. "Swing, Gaucho," he boomed. "What do you think you are being paid for!"

The Argentinian leaned into the suspended ball, took a monumental cut that sent him spinning to the ground like a twisted pretzel. He had missed. The ball gently floated over the swing and popped into the catcher's mitt. The catcher—a fourth-string rookie they all called "Buster"—dropped his mitt and ball and ran howling into the dressing room mumbling something about "Martians" and "space creeps." It took quite an effort to calm him down.

"Do you guys want to see more?" Wires cooed.

They did not. Johnny was signed to a comfortable contract and a $100,000 bonus. He was sent to Tidewater, the

Mets classy minor-league club, for some seasoning with strict orders not to unveil his strange abilities to anyone, at any time, in any game until the front office figured out how to handle the hottest property ever to appear in organized baseball—at least according to all the records. Johnny pitched mediocre baseball during his short stay with Tidewater. He won a few games and lost a few. He never completed a game and excited no one.

The Mets meanwhile had a good season and won their division pennant. Now they faced the Chicago Cubs, the Western Division champions, for the National League's World Series crown. The city of Chicago was wild with joy. It finally had a winner. For their part, the Cubs were supremely confident that Lady Luck was riding with them and that they would emerge world champions in the best out of seven games series, especially since the first two games were to be played at Wrigley Field in the open air before a live home-town crowd.

The Mets quietly brought up Johnny Noonan from their Tidewater farm club. The unknown, untested young pitcher with a lackluster minor-league record was given the starting assignment for the second game of the series. The Mets wanted to see what they could do without their psychokinetic pitcher in the first game. Moreover, they wanted to make sure that Johnny could still work his "magic" before they made fools out of themselves.

While the Mets were in the process of losing the first game 5–1 before the roaring, cheering, celebrating Chicago populace, Johnny was secretly demonstrating to the Mets brass that he had not lost his touch.

"Oh, the marvel of that boy," the Met president, J. Phelps Wiggington, gleefully thought as the vision of the New York Mets' permanent leadership in the baseball world danced in his head.

74

The next day all Chicago watched with astonishment as an unheralded fifteen-year-old gangly kid from Brooklyn calmly crushed their wonderful Cubs in his first major-league appearance—the second game of a World Series, no less. Johnny Noonan's performance was the weirdest exhibition of pitching ever seen. He did not do wild things with the ball. He simply moved the ball over, under, and around the swinging Cub bats, just enough for them to miss, not enough for either the players or the fans to suspect anything unusual. He threw exactly eighty-one pitches—three pitches to twenty-seven batters—and struck out every man he faced. It was a perfect game—the most perfect game ever played —in which the Mets finished on top to even the series. The final score was 1–0.

The series moved to Shea Ballstudio in the borough of Queens, New York. Johnny did not start the third game but was held in reserve should he be needed. The Mets won easily over the demoralized Cubs, 7–2. The Mets were never in trouble. The Cubs scored their two runs on their only hits— two homers. That was it. The Mets had a one-game edge. The following day they made it a two-game edge by beating the Cubs. They needed one more victory to wrap up the World Series.

"This is it, Johnny, the clincher," his manager, Imogene Gibson, told him as she trotted out to play second base. "Do your thing."

Johnny did his thing in the fifth and final game of the 1996 National League World Series. He destroyed the Chicago Cubs in the same calm manner he demonstrated in the second game. The twenty-seven Cubs he faced were reduced to a bunch of ineffectual, whimpering bush leaguers. Johnny Noonan became an instant immortal. His place in the Hall of Fame at Cooperstown, New York, was assured. He had pitched two back-to-back perfect games. The only other

pitcher ever to do that was Johnny Vander Meer who performed the rarity for Cincinnati on June 11 and June 15, 1938. The only difference was that Vander Meer did not strike out everyone, every time, and the games were not played during a World Series.

In a fit of pique and utter frustration, the Wrigleys, who had come so far only to lose the "big one"—the series—and who had held out so long to keep baseball traditional and outdoors, sold the Cubs to a Salt Lake City syndicate who made preparations to move the team to Utah, where it would play as the Salt Lake City Cubs. Also, they turned Wrigley Field over to the National Trust permanently on the condition that only old-timers' games be played there frequently on a regular schedule. An Old-timers' League was formed giving both retired ballplayers and umpires something to do. The gift made a living museum out of Wrigley Field.

Within an hour following their final win over Chicago, Shea Ballstudio was a shambles. Thousands of fans left their homes, taverns, and TV sets and descended on the studio. They tore it apart, demanding, while celebrating, a ball park where they could watch Superstar Johnny Noonan in person.

The Mets management stopped the rampaging crowd before it turned into the ugly mobs that jarred Chicago, the nation, and the world in the now famous Chicago Baseball Riots by announcing plans to build a ninety-thousand-seat stadium in Prospect Park, Brooklyn.

"The game belongs to you, the paying fans," exclaimed J. Phelps Wiggington, Mets president. "We are going to give it back to you." The crowd gave a mighty roar of satisfaction and showed their appreciation by finishing the job of leveling Shea Ballstudio to the ground and carting off the outfield artificial turf.

"It's time to write my paper—to let the cat out of the bag, as it were—is it not, Wires, my friend?" Dr. Jim Franzheim was eager to present to the world a true psychokinetic, Johnny Noonan.

"Okay, Doc. You're on. The brass says fine. Go ahead. They can't wait to read your paper themselves. In fact they can't wait to see the look on the faces of the rest of the league."

Franzheim wrote his paper, delivered it before the annual conference of the American Association of Psychologists in Atlantic City, and allowed it to be published simultaneously both in that association's journal and in the New York *Times*.

The revelation was shocking and devastating, not at all what the Mets front office, Wires, or Johnny himself anticipated. It sent shock waves around the world, a world now fearful that such awesome power in the hands of a fifteen-year-old "jock" could bring global anarchy, political unrest —even war.

U.S. News & World Report featured a cover story, "United States Demonstrates Peaceful Uses of Psychokinetic Power."

Both *Time* and *Newsweek* rushed to the stands with articles proclaiming American invincibility, "Balance of Power Swings to U.S." and "Baseball New U.S. Secret Weapon."

The rest of the world shivered with apprehension. Russian reaction was quick. Two of their agents, one of whom was the bull-pen catcher for the Mets, the other the Cubs' right fielder, had been warning the Kremlin about the "Noonan Connection." Hoping to neutralize the American advantage and give the Chinese something to think about, the Russians revealed to the world that they, too, had a psychokinetic—a basketball player from Smolensk, one Gregor Iganovich. The Chinese were taken completely by surprise. None of the agents from their espionage apparatus played for either the Cubs or the Mets. Within fifteen minutes of the Russian announcement the People's Republic of China broadcasted that they had a psychokinetic juggler but refused to give his name, stating only that he was traveling with the People's Circus on the Tibetan border.

Johnny Noonan jolted the American press into action.

The Washington *Post* bawled, "Foul!" and demanded a Senate investigation.

The New York *Daily News* headline was simple: "Let's Go Mets!"

The Los Angeles *Times* minced no words: "Hoax?" they wanted to know on the front page.

The Dallas *Star* proclaimed, "All Power to America!"

The Cleveland *Press* yelled, "Play Ball!"

The Yale Daily News: "Let's Hear It for Noonan."

The Christian Science Monitor: "Who is John Noonan?"

A storm of protest swept the National League. Players threatened to strike or quit the game altogether if something was not done to stop Johnny Noonan. The owners railed against Met "witchery" and insisted the World Series was "illegal." The Cubs—now the Salt Lake City Cubs—demanded that the Commissioner of Baseball force the Mets to give up the championship and have themselves declared champs by default or forfeit—it made no difference to them which it was. Barring that, the Cubs wanted to replay the entire series without "that psycho."

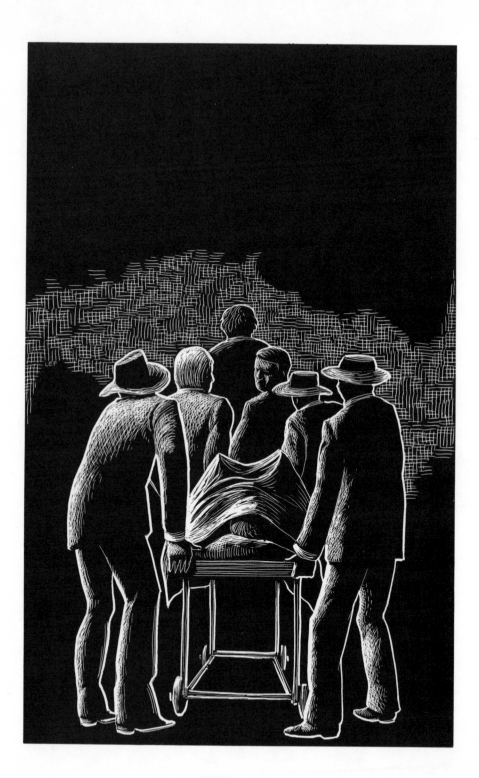

The Mets kept their silence. They went into hiding and issued no statements. The commissioner and his staff were locked in a hotel room in Washington, D.C., with the club owners trying to work things out. In New York the United Nations took up the debate with respect to the dangerous international complications. The Security Council listened attentively and politely to the American ambassador explain the fine points of the national pastime. The Indian ambassador interrupted him several times to say that America's children would be better off if they learned how to play cricket, a much more civilized sport. The council adjourned to listen to a news conference called by the commissioner.

"I've been fired," was his only comment. The council returned to the debate.

Johnny Noonan, accompanied by Wires Marconi, Jerry Koosman, Dr. Franzheim, and a three-man twenty-four-hour guard, was sent to Baltimore to hide until everything blew over. The Mets rented a private room in Johns Hopkins Hospital figuring that no one would ever find their ace pitcher there. They all went in disguise. Johnny was carried into the hospital and up to his room on a stretcher. He was buried under a blanket so that no one would suspect who he was or question his right to be in a hospital.

The guards remained outside the room. The door was locked. Johnny bolted off the stretcher and flopped on a bed. He eyed Marconi, Koosman, and Franzheim with creeping apprehension.

"What's this place?" Johnny asked his three companions. "What am I doing here?"

15.

"What's this place? What am I doing here?" Johnny had finally opened his eyes and glanced around with suspicion. It was 6:20 P.M. He had been unconscious about four hours and ten minutes.

"Easy does it, Johnny. Easy does it," O'Brien whispered. "You are in the hospital."

"Hospital!"

"You've had a nasty whack on the head, son," his father, Mike, chimed in. "But it looks like you are on the mend now."

"Oh yes. I remember. Eastman was up and he . . ."

"Well, Johnny," the doctor interrupted, "welcome back. How do you feel?"

"Great! When do I get out of here? And who won?"

III.

Time is an endless fall
   or stall.
Time is for playing
   or delaying.
Time is the umpire's call:
   "New ball!"

1.

"Don't burn 'em in yet, Johnny," Mike cautioned his son. "Just loosen up. Relax. Throw the ball nice and easy. That's it. Nice and easy."

Johnny and the Dutchmen were back in Brooklyn on the corner of Utica and Remsen avenues after their unfortunate appearance in Baltimore. The first game of a two-game series with the Dover Cavaliers was in the sixth inning before a thin crowd of some one hundred. The Dutchmen were out in front by eleven runs, 12–1.

Johnny Noonan was in the bull pen behind the left-field fence casually exercising his arm. He had been up and down all through the game testing his form. He had spent several days in the Baltimore hospital before being discharged and several days more at home impatiently resting. Doctor's orders. All this seemed more precautionary than anything else. Although he had been unconscious for better than four hours, Johnny Noonan seemed none the worse for wear. He showed no aftereffects whatever. He was alert, bright, optimistic, and eager to get back into uniform. He had no vision problems, which could often result from a severe head blow; no dizziness; no lumps; no dents; and surely no loss of appetite. As it turned out, he did not even have a skull fracture as was first supposed.

"The young man," said the doctor, "has an iron head."

85

Now Johnny Noonan was where he belonged—at the ball park, in uniform, on a pitcher's mound.

"I'm fine, Dad. Let me breeze in a few, will you?"

"Not today. Tomorrow. Maybe. If you do it my way, you'll start against Cincinnati. Remember Cincinnati?"

Johnny remembered Cincinnati. So did O'Brien as he watched his Dutchmen easily defeat the Cavaliers. O'Brien had Cincinnati very much on his mind. He had for years. Now that Johnny's ordeal seemed to be over and he was up and throwing in the bull pen, O'Brien's confidence was soaring. The season did not look as bleak as it did the moment Jack Eastman's foul ball smashed into Johnny's skull. The near bankrupt Continental League seemed to perk up with Johnny back in uniform. The exhibition game with Cincinnati would go on as scheduled in another week and half. The chance that Johnny would start that game looked good. Win or lose, O'Brien felt that he and his Dutchmen could only improve their status in Brooklyn, in organized baseball, and in Seth Low's heart.

If the impossible should happen—if the Dutchmen should beat Cincinnati—O'Brien and his boys could go on to greater glory while the Continental League could possibly emerge as a recognized major league on a par with the Nationals.

"If the worst should happen," O'Brien told Mike Noonan, "and we should lose, our league will disappear like a ball of dust."

"What about the Dutchmen?"

"Well, I've given that some thought. We'll probably be honored in defeat in Brooklyn. Seth Low will see to that. And with all the Van Siclen money behind us—we are about the richest club in baseball, you know—that Van Siclen money comes out of a bottomless well—we'll be invited to join the National League. And this time I'll take

86

them up on it. Any way you look at it, Mike, out star is going to shine."

"I hope you are right, Charlie."

2.

Two days later Johnny was in the bull pen as he had been when the Dutchmen beat Dover 12–1 followed by a 4–3 loss. He was throwing easily to Joe Barlowe, the Dutchmen catcher. O'Brien watched. It was an off day. No game was scheduled. Mike Noonan was at home plate fungoing fly balls to a group of players in right field.

"How does he look?" O'Brien asked his burly catcher.

"Not bad, boss. The kid is pitching to the mitt every time. No hesitation. Very smooth. Why don't you let him bear down a little? I think he's getting bored. Let's see how he does."

"Okay, Johnny. You heard the man. Let one rip."

"You mean it?"

"You heard him," Barlowe barked.

Johnny walked around the mound, shook his shoulders, picked up some dirt, and stepped to the rubber. He rocked and whipped his arm around with all of his strength. The ball got away from him and shot wildly toward his right. It traveled about thirty-five or forty feet when it abruptly changed direction and landed in the startled Barlowe's mitt. He stared at the ball, at Johnny, at O'Brien, who was as popeyed as he was.

"Did you see that, boss!"

"What the devil *was* that?" O'Brien wanted to know.

"I dunno," replied Johnny, who seemed to be as stupefied as Barlowe and O'Brien. "I just told the ball to get back in there. And it did!"

"You what!"

"The kid spoke to the ball, boss!"

"Nonsense. That's got to be the most sensational curve I have ever seen."

"That was no curve, boss," Barlowe corrected him. "That was an angle. First time I ever seen anything like it!"

"Me too," said Johnny.

"Do it again," O'Brien commanded the young pitcher.

"I'll have to throw it wild on purpose this time, Charlie."

"Are you telling me that angle pitch or whatever it was, was a wild pitch with a little quick abracadabra thrown in to set it right?"

"I sure didn't mean for it to go sailing out of my hand like that. I lost my grip on it and it got away from me. Like I said, I told the thing to get back in there."

"Listen, Johnny. I don't know what you did. But whatever it was, do it again."

Johnny whipped about a three-quarter speed ball to his right—not as far to his right as the previous pitch. This time he aimed a controlled pitch at an invisible spot some six feet to the left of the plate. Had there been a right-handed batter in the box, the ball would have been coming at his back. Barlowe quickly shifted over to grab the apparently wild pitch. He never caught it. The ball took a sharp turn in direction toward the left—about a seventy-five-degree course correction. It zipped in over the plate and hit a backstop fence twenty feet beyond. Had there been an umpire present he would have called the pitch a strike. Barlowe was speechless. The astonished O'Brien asked Johnny if he had "spoken" to the ball.

"Yup. I told it to get back in there. Same as before."

"Good Lord!" was all that O'Brien could manage. "Don't

throw another ball until I get back. I want Mike to see this. And I think we ought to have a batter."

O'Brien started to run across the left-field grass but suddenly thought better of it. He did not want to attract any unnecessary attention. He reached Mike after a lazy stroll across the field and asked Mike to join him in the bull pen. He then motioned to Nate Franks, the peppery, clutch-hitting shortstop, to follow. No one paid the slightest attention to the three men sauntering toward the bull pen.

O'Brien said nothing until they reached Barlowe and Johnny.

"Okay, Nate. Step in there. Put a little wood on the ball."

When Nate Franks was out of earshot, O'Brien took Mike by the arm and told him he was going to see something he'll never believe. He then walked to the mound and instructed Johnny to throw Franks a couple of balls he could hit and then "go to work on him."

Johnny did as he was told. He threw Nate Franks a couple of balls that he could meet and tap back to the mound. Johnny did not know quite what to do next. Nate stood there waiting, professionally confident, his bat cocked halfway back ready to punch another ground ball back at Johnny. Johnny knew he would have to "speak" to the ball but decided to use his imagination—to do something different.

Johnny wound up and fired an overhand fast ball at Franks—the first overhand fast ball the sidearmer had ever thrown. Franks saw that the ball was streaking straight for the plate and would come in about waist-high. He drew his bat farther back, instinctively timed the pitch, and got set to bang it. As the ball reached a spot some three or four inches in front of the plate it stopped. It was as if it had hit an invisible wall. Franks swung as the suspended ball fell to the ground. He missed.

"What the h——"

"Did you see that, Mike? Did you see it? Do you believe it?"

"I saw it, Charlie. But I don't believe it."

"Throw a few more, Johnny. Maybe then your old man will believe it. He speaks to the ball, Mike. That's how he does it. He speaks to it!"

Johnny threw a dozen more pitches that did strange things including one pitch that stopped in front of the plate, reversed itself, coming halfway back to Johnny and then, reversing itself a second time, streaked across the plate as Franks watched it go by. Johnny was plainly enjoying his new-found power. Finally O'Brien called it a day, pledging everyone present—Mike, Barlowe, Franks, Johnny, and himself—to absolute secrecy.

"We are going to give Cincinnati something to remember," he told them.

Later that same day Mike insisted that Johnny tell him the secret of his fantastic pitches. Johnny had no answer.

"It's impossible, Johnny, to do what you did with a baseball!"

"I know. It's crazy. But I did it, Dad, so it cannot be impossible. You saw it yourself. So did O'Brien, Barlowe, and Franks!"

"Maybe we all *thought* we saw the ball do tricks."

"How can that be? I threw the ball, told it what I wanted it to do—in my mind, of course—and then stared after it real hard."

"There has got to be more to it. And I wish you'd tell me. I'm your father. Maybe it was the way you gripped the ball. I know it wasn't the ball. We took them all apart."

"I tell you, Dad, I threw them like always. But, you know, it's a funny thing . . ."

"What's a funny thing?"

"I have a strange feeling that I've done it before, someplace else. I can't put my finger on it. It's just a feeling that won't go away—like a tune that gets stuck in your head. Were you ever in a place for the very first time and felt you've been there before?"

"Sure. Most people get that sensation every so often."

"Well, that's what this is like. Every time I threw those crazy balls, I felt I had thrown them all before."

"I think that knock on your head did something to your arm."

3.

The Brooklyn Dutchmen, led by Charlie O'Brien, boarded their train in New York anxious to prove their worth in Cincinnati. O'Brien's only fear was that Johnny Noonan would lose his "stuff." If Johnny still had the "magic," as he put it, then the outcome of this exhibition game was in the bag—the Dutchmen's bag. Johnny was silent, impassive, and tormented during the overnight trip. Much depended upon him. Now that the moment of truth was at hand he was not altogether sure he liked the responsibility.

"What if the ball doesn't behave," he kept muttering to himself over and over again.

Barlowe and Franks, both of whom were sworn to secrecy, had all to do to keep their mouths shut. O'Brien hovered over them like a worried guardian angel making sure they did just that—kept their mouths shut.

All during the ride, Mike Noonan was restless, unable to come to terms with his son's new way with a baseball.

"It just isn't natural," he muttered to himself over and over again.

He wanted to make a connection between Johnny's accident in Baltimore and his strange power over the ball. He reasoned that Johnny did not possess such ability before he was beaned by Eastman's foul. The explanation was in that event someplace. It nagged him. It haunted him. But in the end, it was beyond him, beyond the reality of life as he understood it. It was beyond Johnny, too, for that matter. He had no recollection, no memory of his unconscious flight into the future. He had a new-found gift. But he had no way of knowing it came from the future—from his own far-off bloodline, from his own distant namesake yet to be born.

There were no explanations. It was beyond every living soul.

4.

The Cincinnati welcoming committee—the players, their followers, and the milling crowd of curious travelers—had no trouble spotting the team from the East. "The Brooklyn Dutchmen Baseball Club" leaped at them in white from a navy blue banner that hung from the side of the special car in which the team made the trip. A brass band, resplendent in red and gold uniforms, stood to one side of the assemblage charging the bright day with martial tunes, sending ripples of excitement through the throng.

Finally, when all the Dutchmen had disembarked from their special coach, Buck Ewing, the Red Stockings' first

baseman-manager, stepped forward and presented Charlie O'Brien with a huge floral wreath on behalf of the "good people of the city of Cincinnati." O'Brien accepted the gesture with the stately demeanor of a foreign potentate. As he cleared his throat to make an appropriate acceptance speech, he noticed the inscription on the wreath's banner, "In Memoriam, The Brooklyn Dutchmen, 1896." Charlie took the gesture for what it was—some good-natured ribbing—and burst out laughing, wondering what was next on the program. He did not have long to wait.

A number of Cincinnati players—Dummy Hoy, Farmer Vaughn, Heinie Peitz, Germany Smith, and Eddie Burke—emerged from the crowd. They persuaded Johnny Noonan to stand in the center of a semicircle they had formed. The band struck up the opening chords of "When Johnny Comes Marching Home Again" and the player-choral group proceeded to rasp their hoarse version of the popular tune:

> When Johnny goes marching home again,
>   Hurrah, Hurrah;
> We'll give him a hearty bye-goodbye,
>   Hurrah, Hurrah;
> Our team will cheer, the crowds will shout,
> "Cincinnati has won the bout,"
>   And we'll all feel fine
> When Johnny goes marching home.

The loyal Cincinnati crowd whooped and cheered. The silent Dutchmen refused to go along with the fun. O'Brien was not particularly amused either. They were all indignant that their young pitcher should have been made the target of Cincinnati amusement. Johnny's reaction, however, amazed his teammates. He bowed deeply, dramatically, and shook each of the singer's hands, thanking them for "the

95

honor." With that, the ceremonies were concluded—if that is what they were, ceremonies—and the Brooklyn Dutchmen headed for their hotel.

"What kind of an honor was that?" O'Brien asked Johnny later, referring to his response to the song.

"They'll find out tomorrow, Charlie, when I make them eat those words. They'll be singing a different tune when we leave."

O'Brien went to sleep content and confident. Cincinnati's humor would backfire. The songsters did nothing more than antagonize his ace pitcher. Johnny was determined to work his "magic" on them without mercy.

5.

The field announcer shouting the team line-ups through his megaphone might just as well have been screaming at nothing. The five thousand spectators that packed the stands to see their Cincinnati Red Stockings swamp the team from Brooklyn kept roaring, "Play ball." No one heard the line-ups.

Buck Ewing and Charlie O'Brien presented their batting orders to the umpires at home plate. A brief discussion followed regarding the ground rules. Pirate LaFitte, the Dutchmen's lead-off man, was swinging a couple of bats impatiently awaiting the umpire's signal to begin the game. The home-plate conference ended and Cincinnati took the field to the thunderous cheer of the spectators.

Chauncey Burr Fisher—"Peach" Fisher—was on the mound throwing his warm-up pitches to Farmer Vaughn, the catcher. The choice of Fisher to pitch this exhibition game was a mark of contempt. Fisher was not only the worst pitcher on the Cincinnati roster, he was also one of the poorest pitchers in the National League. He had the highest earned run average in the league—4.50—giving up four or five runs per game every time he pitched. Farmer Vaughn, his battery mate, was a good hitting catcher but second-string. Henry Clement "Heinie" Peitz was Cincinnati's first-string catcher. The rest of the team—Bid McPhee, second base; Germany Smith, shortstop; Charlie Irwin, third base; Dusty Miller, right field; Dummy Hoy, center field; Eddie Burke, left field—were everyday regulars, as was Buck Ewing, first baseman and manager.

"Play ball," Jojo Stewart, the plate umpire, bellowed. The game was on.

Pirate LaFitte stepped in and slammed Fisher's first pitch into center field for a single. Right fielder Harry Dockstetter sacrificed him over to second with a perfect bunt. One out, man on second.

Fisher strolled around the mound, took a deep breath, and steadied himself to face the Brooklyn left fielder, Pete Birns. With a 3–2 count on him Birns fouled off five consecutive pitches before flying out to Dummy Hoy. Two out, man on second. Binks Overstreet, the Dutchmen cleanup batter, stepped in. Like LaFitté, he swung at the first pitch and lined it over third base straight down the legal side of the foul line for a triple. LaFitte scored easily from second. The Dutchmen took a quick lead, 1–0, and the crowded stands were deathly quiet.

Buck Ewing wasted no time with any further marks of contempt. He yanked Fisher out of the game and called for Billy Rhines, the best arm on the Cincinnati pitching staff. He promptly struck out Nate Franks on three successive pitches and restored some Cincinnati confidence. The inning was over and Cincinnati came to bat.

Johnny walked to the mound slowly as the Brooklyn

infield fired the ball back and forth. He threw a half-dozen warm-ups and signaled the umpire that he was ready. Germany Smith stepped into the batter's box.

Johnny Noonan fired an overhand "cannon" ball down the middle. Smith took a healthy cut at the pitch and missed. The ball had taken a sharp left ninety-degree turn several inches in front of the plate and rolled to the Cincinnati bench.

"Steeeeeeeeeeeerike one," Jojo Stewart bawled, holding up one finger. The call echoed around the park like a shrill siren. The crowd moaned. Germany Smith figured he had fouled off the first pitch. So did the umpire, the Cincinnati bench, the crowd, and most of the Dutchmen. The smiling O'Brien, the Noonans, Joe Barlow, and Nate Franks knew otherwise.

Smith stepped back in the box. Johnny put his foot on the rubber, rocked, swung around, and whipped the second pitch in with his familiar sidearm motion. The ball streaked for the plate in a wide looping arc. About midway it crossed between Johnny and the batter and headed for the first-base line. Johnny stared at the ball. It reversed itself and made another looping arc toward the plate sweeping across letter-high—in the strike zone.

Germany Smith was still gaping at the reverse "S" route the ball had taken as the astonished Jojo Stewart called, Steeeeeeeeeeeerike two!" Barlowe laughed so hard he fell to his knees. "That's talking to the ball, kid," he giggled.

Cincinnati manager Buck Ewing was off the bench like a shot.

"Did you see that, Jojo? Was that legal?"

"Yeah. I saw it, Buck. But I don't believe it."

"I don't believe it either. And if you don't believe it then it's an illegal pitch. Illegal, I tell you!"

"Hey. Hold on there. Who's the umpire here? You or

98

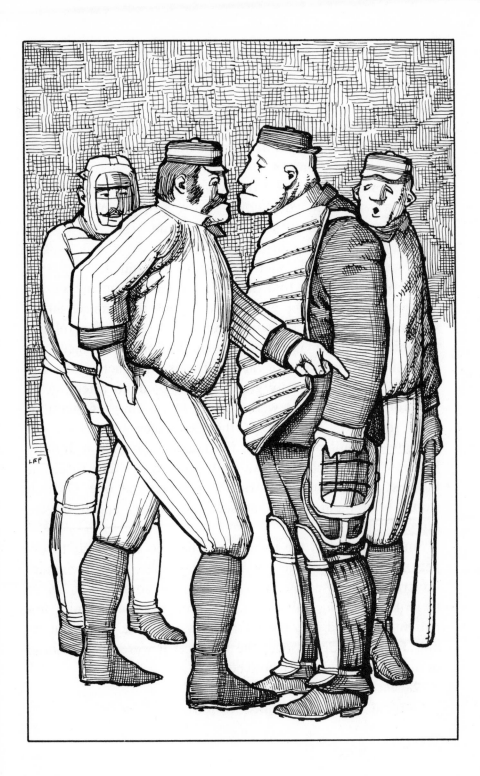

me? I didn't say it was illegal. I just said I didn't believe it."

"It's illegal!" Ewing insisted.

The two men stood jaw to jaw, eyeball to eyeball.

"It came over the plate, didn't it? I called it, didn't I?"

"That's not the point! That—that—double curve—or whatever it was—was an il——"

"Sit down, Buck, or I'll throw you out of the game. It's a little early for that, you know. You've still got nine innings to go. Your boy has got two strikes on him."

Ewing kicked some dirt and sat down.

"I want a new ball," Germany Smith demanded.

"New ball!" cried Jojo Stewart. He fished one out of his oversize jacket pocket and tossed it out to Johnny. Smith stepped back in the box once more and waited for Johnny to finish rubbing up the new ball. Johnny glanced at O'Brien, who was sitting on the Brooklyn bench along the third-base line peacefully grinning. He paid no attention to the stormy clouds that were closing in on sunny Cincinnati from the west. The rest of the Dutchmen—those on the field, in the bull pen, and on the bench—gawked at Johnny Noonan with trancelike awe and wonder, waiting to see if the next pitch would be as rare as the previous one. O'Brien would brief them all just as soon as Johnny ended the inning.

Smith, behind in the count 0–2, had no idea what to expect from Johnny. The young pitcher threw him a change-up straight as an arrow. The ball traveled so slowly it began to look like a big balloon as it neared the plate. Smith impatiently stepped into the pitch. How could he miss? But he did. The ball skipped over the bat as if it were on a cushion of air. The crowd never noticed.

"Steeeeeeeeeeeerike three. Yer out."

One out. Barlowe pounded his mitt.

100

Second baseman Bid McPhee stepped into the batter's box. He looked up at the sky and wondered how long it would be before some rain fell on them.

"Okay, McPhee," Barlowe said, "let's see how good you are."

McPhee, a consistent .300 hitter, snarled and cocked his bat menacingly.

Johnny, growing more confident, threw a halfhearted pitch that curved down and away from McPhee. McPhee let it go by. He was not about to be taken by the first throw.

"Ball one," roared Jojo Stewart.

Barlowe walked the ball back to the mound. "You okay, kid?"

"Sure, Joe. I knew he wouldn't swing at the first pitch."

"Listen, kid, from now on, don't be sure of nothin'. We'll do the thinking. You do the throwing. Strikes. You got that? All strikes! Just talk to the ball, kid. Make 'em all do tricks. Work the ball! Don't pitch."

Johnny threw the ball. It dipped and danced all around McPhee's bat. He never swung at a ball. He went down looking at Johnny's strikes. The crowd, suspecting nothing, sighed quietly.

Two out. Barlowe spit in his mitt and pounded it some more.

William Ellsworth "Dummy" Hoy, the five-foot-four-inch, 148-pound, .300 slugging center fielder, came to the plate.

"Watch this, Barlowe."

Barlowe watched as Hoy fanned on three consecutive pitches that lurched away from him and his swinging bat.

Three out.

Charlie O'Brien let the cat out of the bag. He told his club about Johnny Noonan's magical power over a pitched ball. "Someday, somewhere, someone will figure out how and why. Then they'll invent a name for it. Right now we are going to beat these guys and have the record show it—exhibition game or not."

All of the Dutchmen said the obvious, "If we hadn't seen it with our own eyes, we wouldn't have believed it."

"Cincinnati thought we would be a push-over. Now they are not so sure. In fact they are not sure of anything. Just play it straight and stay alert." Charlie was in command—king of the jungle—a lion stalking his prey—setting him up for the kill. "Barlowe," he growled. "You're up."

The sun disappeared behind the ominous clouds. The day darkened. Joe Barlowe walked. One on. Jack Eastman, now back in Charlie O'Brien's good graces, popped up to Charlie Irwin at third base. Barlowe stayed where he was. One out. Man on first. Amos Stone, third baseman, slapped the ball back to the mound. Billy Rhines fired it to Germany Smith covering second for the force out on Barlowe. Two away. Smith pegged the ball to Buck Ewing at first for an easy double play. Three up. Three down. The Dutchmen were still ahead 1–0 as Cincinnati came to bat in the bottom half of the second inning.

It started to drizzle. Johnny took a few warm-up throws. Eddie Burke, the heavy-hitting left fielder, came to the plate. Johnny threw him a straight fast ball that rose high in the air and out of the park behind home plate as Burke came around with his bat.

"Steeeeeeeeeeeerike one!"

Everyone in the park, including the umpire, thought that Burke had actually fouled the ball off; everyone, that is, except the Dutchmen. They knew that the bat never touched the ball. It made little difference. Burke had taken a cut and missed.

The drizzle turned into a downpour. Johnny went into his motion. He never delivered the ball. Jojo Stewart stopped

102

the action temporarily, hoping to resume play within the half hour when and if the rain passed over.

6.

The count was no balls and one strike on Cincinnati's Eddie Burke when the game continued a half hour later. The sky was still overcast, still threatening, but at least dry for the moment. The rain had gone away and so had the drenched crowd. The stands were empty. The two teams were now about to play to an empty house.

A small canvas had covered the mound and the home plate areas to keep them dry. The rest of the playing field was exposed to the weather. The infield had become a muddy ooze. The outfield was a swamp.

"How are we going to play ball on this field?" the Dutchmen asked O'Brien.

"You are not expected to play. Only Johnny and Barlowe need to play. If a little mud bothers you," he said to Eastman, LaFitte, and Stone, "stand on the bases. The rest of you find some high ground. Don't bother none about positioning. No one is going to hit anything to anyone. Right, Johnny?"

"Right."

Johnny stepped on the rubber, rocked, turned, and side-armed a pitch that zigzagged its way to the plate. Burke followed the ball's angular route with his head, snapping it from side to side with every zig and every zag. The ball crossed the plate and landed in the hysterically laughing

Barlowe's mitt. Burke never moved his bat. Burke was wild-eyed, unbelieving.

"Steeeeeeeeeeeerike two," Jojo Stewart barked.

Barlowe backed away and staggered around holding his sides, laughing like a crazy man. O'Brien rushed over to him. "Shut up, you idiot, or you'll spill the beans."

Ewing was off the bench again demanding to see the ball. Barlowe tossed it to Stewart, who examined it first before handing it over to the Cincinnati manager. "It's just an ordinary ball, Buck," the umpire declared. "See for yourself."

Ewing looked at it, turned it over and over, and finally rolled it back to the bench. "Take it apart," he ordered. "Let's have a new ball, Jojo."

"New ball!" cried Jojo Stewart, tossing it out to Johnny.

As Johnny rubbed up the new ball, the Cincinnati bench was dissecting the old ball with a hunting knife. They found nothing unusual inside. They turned their attention to the Dutchman pitcher and watched him intently.

"No one can do to a baseball what that kid is doing," Ewing muttered. "It's a trick of some kind. It's got to be."

Johnny flipped the ball in his hand nonchalantly and looked at Burke. The batter had not moved an inch, not a muscle. He stared vacantly out at the field. He seemed to be made of cement.

Ewing screamed at him. "Burke! Wake up!"

Burke shuddered as if someone had pushed a start button in his head and began to pump his bat with the same old menace. Johnny threw him a three-quarter speed ball and hung it right at the front edge of the plate three feet aboveground. Burke started to swing but stopped. The ball moved forward and plopped into Barlowe's mitt.

"Steeeeeeeeeeeerike three! Yer out! One away!"

Burke, a .340 hitter with great respect around the National League, stood motionless, his eyes glazed.

Ewing was off the bench again. "That's illegal, Jojo. That ball stopped."

"It moved again, didn't it?"

"Yeah. But . . ."

"No buts about it, Buck. I'd say that was a hesitation pitch. Very legal."

"Hesitation pitch! Where did you ever see a hesitation pitch before?"

"Just a minute ago."

"Bah! I'm officially informing you, Jojo, that we are playing this game under protest!"

"Protest! You can't protest a nonleague game."

"There's nothing in the rules that says I can't!"

The two men were at it again, jaw to jaw, eyeball to eyeball. The entire Cincinnati bench was on its collective feet behind their manager. The Dutchmen watched the spectacle quietly, amused, untroubled. The sky darkened again. A low peal of thunder rippled across the western outskirts of Cincinnati.

"What good is a protest? This is an exhibition game."

"That's not the point, you big tub of lard, that kid out there is a menace to baseball. He ain't human. He's some kinda spook. Maybe we ought to take *him* apart like we did that ball."

"Who did you call a big tub of lard?"

"You, you big tub of lard!"

"You're out of the game! *O–U–T!* Out! If you aren't off this field and your boys nice and peaceful-like on the bench in five seconds, you'll forfeit the game. And how would that look in the papers. You'd have a lot of explaining to do to the commissioner, too. And he won't believe a word of it! Out! Big tub of lard, am I! Who's acting manager?"

"I am," declared Heinie Peitz, Cincinnati's number-one catcher and another .300 hitter. "Farmer Vaughn is out. I'm in as of right now." Peitz stepped into the batter's box. "You're not gonna spook me, Noonan. Throw it!"

Johnny threw. Again he hung the ball at the front edge of the plate about three feet aboveground. Peitz stared at the stationary ball, then at Johnny, then at the ball again. Johnny stood relaxed on the mound waiting-for Peitz to do something. The Cincinnati players, glued to their bench with hypnotic fascination, gaped at the incredible sight along with Heinie Peitz. Not even Charlie O'Brien and his Dutchmen could hide their astonishment at a ball suspended in mid-air supported by nothing. Mike Noonan and the bullpen crowd had raced across the field to get a better look when they realized what was going on.

Peitz slowly circled the ball. Seemingly satisfied, he settled himself back in the batter's box and carefully measured his swing against the motionless target. Finally, he brought his big bat around with a mighty swing and walloped the air. The ball jumped above the bat and sailed into Barlowe's waiting glove.

Jojo Stewart began to call the pitch. His mouth dropped open and stayed there. A clap of thunder broke over the field and shook the earth. A bolt of lightning streaked across the center-field sky.

"Well?" asked Barlowe, waiting for the bewildered umpire to call the pitch.

"I guess it's a strike," he whispered.

"Steeeeeeeeeeeerike one," yelled Barlowe in imitation of the umpire and flung the ball back to Johnny.

It started to drizzle again. A hazy, unnatural midafternoon gloom descended on the field.

Johnny threw again. The ball rose and fell in great loops, something like a roller coaster ride at a country fair. Peitz, his fury growing, took a harmless swipe at the ball and felt

106

nothing but the breeze of his swing. The ball had looped under the bat.

"What do you call that, Jojo?" Barlowe demanded.

"Another strike, I suppose." Stewart was becoming increasingly uncertain. The game of baseball, professionally played had certain reasonable limits as spelled out in the rule book. But this—this pitching fantasy he was witnessing —was beyond the rule book. In fact it was beyond reason, explanation, tradition, and human experience. Maybe Buck Ewing was right after all. Maybe this whole thing was illegal. It was certainly unnatural.

"You suppose?" Barlowe retorted. "You better believe it!"

"Seeing isn't always believing," Jojo Stewart mumbled.

"Steeeeeeeeeeeerike two!" Barlowe joyously screamed, running the ball out to Johnny and handing it to him personally. "I don't know how you do it, kid. But do it again. These guys don't know what's happening!"

Johnny threw a change-up. It floated in, lazily, and came to a dead stop letter-high, a foot in front of the plate. Peitz looked pleadingly at Stewart. Stewart shrugged as if to say What can I do about it?

"Come on, Heinie," Barlowe needled him. "Give it a try."

Peitz took a whack at the ball. Missed. The ball jumped back. Peitz chased it. The ball jumped back another foot. Peitz went after it. He tried to club it but the ball danced away from his bat and headed back to the plate. Peitz, now halfway between the mound and home plate, pursued the elusive baseball with blinding rage. With one last desperate effort to nick the ball, he stuck his bat out and lunged. He fell sprawling on the drenched turf as the ball innocently crossed the plate—a perfect strike.

"Let's hear it, Jojo," Barlowe gleefully barked.

"No pitch! The count stands. No balls. Two strikes. The batter wasn't in the box."

"Okay, Johnny. One more time," the catcher ordered.

The rain was falling in sheets. Visibility was poor. It seemed more like evening than midafternoon. Jojo Stewart quickly conferred with the other umpires. They had had enough. Jojo leaned over Heinie Peitz still stretched out on his stomach in front of home plate.

"I'm calling the game, Heinie. It's senseless to go on. We can't see any more. And I'm not sure what I'm seeing anyway. This whole thing is too strange. Come on, you'd better get up from there or you'll drown." Jojo motioned to a couple of Cincinnati players to tend to their acting manager. They came over and dragged him out of the puddle.

Stewart then informed O'Brien that the game was over. "Rain, darkness, and too many shenanigans," he said. "I think we are all better off forgetting anything happened here."

Charlie was upset—frustrated. The Dutchmen had come all the way to Cincinnati only to be rained out after only one and a half innings. A long-time dream had disappeared in a clap of thunder and a bolt of lightning. There was nothing he could do about it except to hope that Cincinnati would someday reschedule the game. But that, he knew, was hardly likely. By the time Charlie O'Brien had wiped the rain out of his eyes, he and his team were alone on the field, soaked and disappointed.

"We gave them something to remember," he shouted to his team above the storm that pounded them where they stood. "And we had them beat, too, one–nothing."

True. Charles Patrick O'Brien, Johnny Noonan, and the Brooklyn Dutchmen Baseball Club gave the Cincinnati Red Stockings something to remember. But the game—such as it was—would never reach the record books. It had ended before four and a half innings had been played—the required number of innings to make it official—exhibition or not. To all intents and purposes and according to National League rules, the game, having been called after one and a half completed innings, had never been played.

That night, as O'Brien packed his bag for the rail trip back to Brooklyn the following morning, Buck Ewing paid him a visit.

"Charlie," he began, "I don't know what your other players are like. Maybe I don't want to know. If they are anything like Noonan—how old did you say he was, fifteen? —they have got to be the devil's own army. Anyway, Noonan is bad for baseball. If he's allowed to continue in the game doing what we think he did, he'll destroy our profession. No one will ever be able to hit him. Strong men will weep and crumble. It'll be no contest."

"That remains to be seen, Buck."

"Have it your way. But that is not what I came here to tell you. I came here to tell you that me and my boys have sworn on the Holy Word never to admit that your boy, Johnny Noonan, did anything superhuman or unnatural to a baseball. The record books won't show anything. The ball park was empty of witnesses. We'll deny that anything out of the ordinary took place here this afternoon. You spooked us—how, I don't know—and you would have gone on spooking us. But so far as we are concerned, it never happened.

"You forget, Buck, the umpires saw the whole thing."

"That's the next thing I have to tell you. Jojo Stewart told me that since rules prevented him from coming up here, he wanted you to know that the umpires will deny the strange occurrences."

"Well, Buck, no one can prevent my boys from describing the meeting with your Red Stockings. And what's more,

110

we've still got Johnny, who can prove it all just by throwing a baseball."

"Maybe so. But he never did it in Cincinnati!"

7.

No one came to the station to see the Dutchmen leave Cincinnati. And only one person saw them arrive home—Seth Low.

"I received your wire, Charlie, my friend. It was very cryptic. Quite mysterious. What did you mean 'won but no win'?"

"Simple. We had them one–nothing going into the bottom of the second inning. The game was called on account of rain and darkness. But you should have seen Johnny. He was unbelievable. They couldn't touch him."

But Charlie was depressed. The team was unable to bring home a decisive finish to their game with Cincinnati. In Charlie's mind, the game did produce a small moral victory —they were ahead when the rain and darkness put an end to the proceedings. They would have stayed ahead, too, or at least as long as Johnny had his "stuff." And by the looks of him he seemed able to go on like that forever. But O'Brien knew the realities. The whole affair was a fiasco. The Brooklyn Dutchmen proved nothing to no one but themselves—and that for less than two innings. If anything, they succeeded in terrorizing a respected team in the National League, making them look foolish at the same time. And that was not a wise thing to do.

Now the city of New York could not be humbled by an

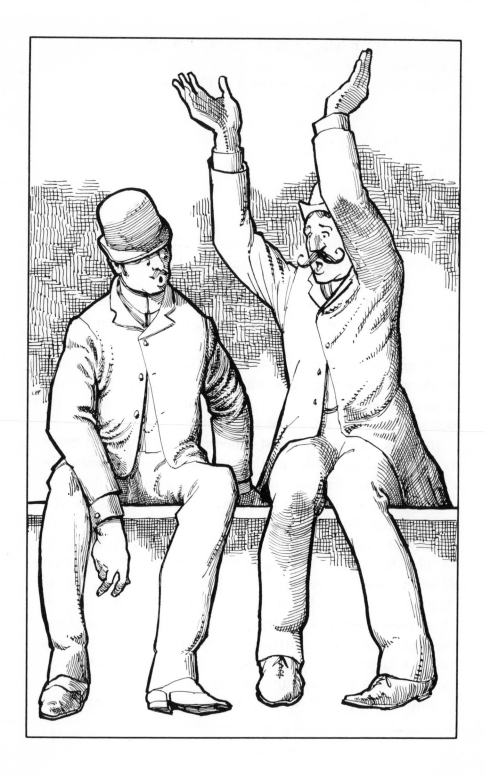

aborted baseball game that would never appear in the record books. The city of Brooklyn would have no better image in the mind of the world than it already had before the Cincinnati trip. The Dutchmen, seeking wider recognition for themselves and the shaky league they played in were no further ahead than they were before. And Seth Low's grand design for a Greater Brooklyn was destined for the scrap heap. The only bright spot was Johnny Noonan. The future—the glorious future—rested on his right arm.

Charlie described Johnny's strange power to Seth Low as they climbed aboard a horse-drawn trolley car heading for the Brooklyn Bridge. He had never mentioned Johnny's ability to the former mayor, preferring to confine the facts to those on the team who bore witness to it all. Now things were different.

"Johnny is Joshua of the Old Book," O'Brien bragged. "He can make the sun stand still."

"Provided it were made of horsehide, Charlie," Seth Low laughed.

"Oh, wonder of wonders!" exclaimed Seth Low when he had been fully briefed. "The world is full of wonders! What will we have next? A man in full flight soaring through the skies? Yes. That's it! A flying man! Oh, wonder of wonders! Have no fear, Charlie, my dear friend. We no longer need a Cincinnati confrontation to extend our realms—yours and mine. That day is over! We have Johnny Noonan! When will our amazing young man pitch again? I must not miss his extraordinary feats! This is what the American dream is all about!"

"Day after tomorrow. We've got a single game with the Providence Preachers."

8.

The sun was high and bright in the sky as the Dutchmen sprinted onto the field at the corner of Utica and Remsen avenues. The stands were packed. The surrounding streets were jammed with people, carriages, and horses of every description. Seth Low had seen to that. His powers of persuasion on short notice were awesome.

Rumor had it that Johnny Noonan threw nothing but strikes; that no one could hit his devious pitches; that he could make a baseball turn a corner; go up; go down; go backward; go sideways; stand still; do anything he told it to do.

"That is exactly what he did in Cincinnati," proclaimed Seth Low, "and they will not admit it!"

The crowds came to see for themselves. Six thousand delirious people pressed the ball park from every direction to see Brooklyn's own "miracle arm"—an apt description provided by Seth Low. Two thousand three hundred of them managed to get inside the park. The other three thousand seven hundred were turned away by the police supplemented by a regiment of the Coast Artillery.

"Now we'll show them," O'Brien smirked. "How will Cincinnati deny what we did to them, Johnny, after you get through with these Providence fellows? And we've got witnesses. More than two thousand of them sitting in the glorious sunshine. And not a drop of rain in sight."

Johnny stood tall and loose on the mound. He had finished his warm-ups and was ready to throw. He surveyed the festive crowd with cool, arrogant confidence.

114

Studs Rosencranz—the same beefy umpire who had officiated in Baltimore—stood large and foreboding behind the plate.

"Play ball," he howled.

The game was on.

Johnny threw a perfect overhand strike at the plate. Jake Roomer, the Preacher second baseman and lead-off man, let it go by. He wanted to study Johnny's delivery before committing his bat to the ball.

"Steeeeeeeeeeeerike one!"

The crowd roared its approval. Barlowe came out in front of the plate and tossed the ball back to his pitcher. "Don't get foxy, kid. You didn't have anything on that ball. Don't pitch to these guys. Just talk to the ball."

Johnny went into his motion and whipped the ball in at Roomer. Roomer backed off, accidentally nicking the ball with his bat. The ball slammed into Rosencranz' chest protector. The umpire stood like a granite wall. The ball dropped harmlessly to the ground.

"Just like old times, eh, Studs?" Barlowe's needling was an obvious reference to that day in Baltimore Johnny Noonan was decked by a foul ball. "A little higher up and you would have been in dreamland. And we'd roll out the meat wagon for you."

Rosencranz ignored the catcher. "Steeeeeeeeeeeerike two. O and two is the count," he bellowed.

The crowd roared its approval again. This is what they came to see. Strikes. Nothing but strikes.

Barlowe pegged the ball back to the mound. "Talk to it, kid! Talk to it!"

Johnny walked around the mound. Beads of perspiration flecked his forehead. Something was wrong. The ball was not behaving. He shook his head, wiped the sweat from his brow, and stepped on the rubber. He squinted, rocked, and fired the ball at the plate.

Crack!

The ball sailed into the hole between short and third for a clean single. Man on first.

The crowd responded with a thunderous boo. Its vision of the "miracle arm" was shattered. "Just a lapse, my friends. A mere lapse," Seth Low informed the spectators within hearing distance.

"A lapse, my foot," cried O'Brien as he raced to the mound. "What happened, Johnny? That guy hit the ball. He wasn't supposed to do that!"

"I dunno what happened, Charlie. I talked to the ball. But it didn't do what I told it to do."

"Talk louder! Do something!"

"Okay, gentlemen, break it up," Rosencranz boomed. "Let's keep this game moving."

O'Brien went back to the bench. The crowd settled down. Johnny stretched, looked over at Roomer on first base, and stared at Pumpkin Larkin, the Preacher's second hitter and right fielder. Johnny fired the ball. Larkin watched it go by.

"Steeeeeeeeeeeerike one!"

The crowd cheered. O'Brien sighed, "Whew. That's more like it." "Talk to it, kid! Talk to it!" Barlowe pleaded.

Johnny stretched and eyed Roomer still on first. Roomer was taunting Johnny with a big lead. Johnny brought his arms down slowly and hurled the ball at the plate. Larkin took a cut.

Crack!

The crowd was on its feet. So was O'Brien. Second baseman LaFitte hauled the line drive down and doubled Roomer off first base. Two out. O'Brien sat down. "Lucky," he muttered. He did not like what was happening. It was going to be a long afternoon.

Pat Grady, the Preacher's third baseman, stepped into the box. He took the first pitch, swung late, and fouled it into Barlowe's mitt. Three out.

116

The worried O'Brien was temporarily relieved. The inning was over. But there was more to come. Johnny had lost his "stuff." If he did not find it again in the next inning, all would be lost. The looming disaster and humiliation would be insufferable.

The Dutchmen came to the plate and were quickly set down in order. LaFitte struck out. Dockstetter grounded out. Birns flied out. No hits. No runs. No errors. At the end of the first inning the score was 0–0.

Johnny was back on the mound. He did not seem as cool and confident as he was at the game's start. He wiped his hands on his blouse, touched his cap a half-dozen times, took it off, and wiped his forehead with his arm. Barlowe came out to the mound to settle the young pitcher down.

"Play ball!" Rosencranz yelled impatiently.

Disaster struck quickly. Moose Moriarity singled. Chafee and Firestone walked. The bases were loaded with none out. The boos and catcalls were deafening. The mood of the crowd was becoming ugly. Someone ran out onto the field and tried to steal the third-base bag. He was tackled by a policeman and hauled away.

O'Brien leaped from the bench and faced the crowd. He ran up and down pleading for patience. "Give the boy a chance. He won't disappoint you. Give him a chance."

"Aaaaah! Sit down, O'Brien."

Johnny pitched three successive strikes to Dan Billings. One out. The crowd quieted down. Homer Hutchinson stepped in and whacked a short fly ball to deep short—not long enough to send a runner home. No one moved on the base paths. Two out. The crowd was silent, sullen.

Dick Gladstone, pitcher, stepped into the batter's box. He was a good hitting pitcher. He worked the count to three balls and two strikes. Barlowe strolled out to the mound. He took his time. Two Dutchmen pitchers, Dewey Calvert

118

and Roscoe Hawkins, began warming up in the bull pen. Mike Noonan sat down next to O'Brien. Mike was stone-faced, expressionless. O'Brien was shaking slightly.

Barlowe handed the ball to Johnny. "Give it one more try, kid," he said softly. "Talk to the ball." He searched the young pitcher's eyes for an explanation. There was none. Johnny looked away. Barlowe patted him encouragingly on the shoulder and returned to his place behind the batter.

Barlowe squatted. Johnny went into his motion and pitched. Gladstone caught a piece of it and fouled it back. The crowd OOOOOOOed. Gladstone fouled back another pitch. The crowd AAAAAAAed. Johnny fired again.

Crack!

Doomsday!

The ball soared fair and long over the right-field fence.

The spectators froze in their seats as they watched the ball go out of sight and four runners cross the plate. O'Brien ran up and down the first-base line.

"It's a mistake! It's all a mistake! Johnny Noonan can make the sun stand still! He did it in Cincinnati!"

"Throw the bum out of here," boomed a loud chorus of disgruntled fans.

O'Brien grabbed a bat and climbed into the stands after the hooting culprits. The noisy mob spilled out onto the playing field. Both teams fled the onrushing throng. Mike Noonan and a couple of policemen got to Johnny before the crowd did. Mike and Johnny were flung into a hay wagon and driven at a great gallop all the way back to Coney Island.

Seth Low escaped quietly. He walked away from the riot, found his carriage, and went home. He had some decisions to make.

The police and Coast Artillery Regiment, unable to contain the disappointed mob, gave up. They let the riot run its course inside the ball park. The umpires, led by Studs Rosencranz, seeing the insurmountable difficulty in resuming the game, declared that the home team—the Brooklyn Dutchmen—had forfeited the game to Providence. They fled for their lives, vowing never again to officiate in Brooklyn.

The last anyone remembered seeing Charles Patrick O'Brien, owner and manager of the Brooklyn Dutchmen, he was smashing a couple of empty seats with his baseball bat.

9.

The events at the corner of Utica and Remsen avenues in Brooklyn sent shock waves through the Continental League. The Dutchmen, unable to play on their home field—it was in shambles—or anywhere in Brooklyn, lest they place their lives in mortal danger, continued a makeshift schedule out of town without Johnny Noonan and their owner-manager, Charlie O'Brien. Johnny and his father quit the team preferring to remain in Coney Island. There, Mike opened another grand and tinkly saloon, the Flying Dutchmen. Johnny worked in his father's saloon and wistfully thought of what might have been. Neither of them ever mentioned Cincinnati or Johnny's brief encounter with mischievous baseballs.

The morning following the riot Seth Low packed his bags and traveled across the East River to New York. He joined that city's political fraternity and became a popular figure. Wherever his good nature and political instincts took him— fund-raising dinners, political rallies, and other public events —he fervently prayed for the quick incorporation of Brooklyn into the Greater City of New York. Kings County ought

120

to be just that—a county—not a separate city of Brooklyn, he would insist.

"An Empire City for an Empire State," he declared. "That, my friends, is what New York is all about."

In 1902 Seth Low became the ninety-second mayor of the city of New York. Brooklyn had been a borough only four years.

The Brooklyn Dutchmen Baseball Club never recovered. Without the strong hand of Charlie O'Brien to guide the team—his whereabouts were a mystery—and the strange arm of Johnny Noonan, they were booed out of existence before the season ended. The Continental League, unable to cope with the rising tide and fortune of the National League, drifted into oblivion at the same time.

In five years' time, the American League would emerge to challenge successfully the National League's monopoly of the national pastime. In that year, 1901, two reporters from the Brooklyn *Eagle* doing a routine story on a private Long Island mental hospital stumbled across a craggy-faced man with a large handlebar mustache.

"Say, aren't you Charlie O'Brien of the old Brooklyn Dutchmen Baseball Club?"

"Who are you two?"

"We are from the Brooklyn *Eagle* here to do a feature on——"

"I knew it! By george, I knew it! I knew you people would come looking for the truth someday. Yes, I'm Charles Patrick O'Brien. The very same. And let me tell you, that Johnny Noonan was a remarkable young man. He did things with a baseball that defied the laws of nature—of gravity—of reason. He had Cincinnati beaten and begging for mercy with pitches that only the devil himself could have inspired. It was something to see! The ball moved sideways, backward, every which way. It even stopped dead in the air."

122

"No one can do that. You know it as well as we do."

"Bah! You're like all the rest. Ignorant! You think I'm crazy, don't you? No one believed me or my players then and you can't believe me now. But it's the truth I tell you. That Johnny could make a baseball do anything he wanted it to do. The Cincinnati club denied the whole thing. And there were no witnesses. The storm drove them all off. Even the umpires denied what I'm telling you Johnny did. You won't find any of this in the record books either. They all said I was mad. They said my players were mad, too. "Whole cloth," they said. And then Johnny lost the power—lost his stuff—and we couldn't prove anything."

"Tough luck, old-timer."

"Everyone still thinks I'm crazy. That's why I'm in this place. I'm as sane as you are. Maybe saner. But I'm stuck here."

"Sure, Charlie. Take care of yourself."

Charlie O'Brien turned his back on the two reporters and shuffled down the hall.

"What do you think, Al? Do you suppose there is any truth to what he said?"

"Are you serious? If I thought there was any truth to what he said, they'd have to commit me to this loony bin. Naw. The poor guy is cracked. Out of his mind. Too bad. He used to be a good baseball man. They used to say, years ago, that Charlie O'Brien had a great future in the game. It doesn't look that way now, does it?"

"How do they humor guys like O'Brien here? How do these patients spend their time? What are Charlie's activities, for example? Who pays the bills? This might be a good angle for the feature."

The two reporters made inquiries and were taken to the office of Otto Franzheim, Director of Patient Activities.

"Ah, gentlemen, Mr. O'Brien is a troubled man, indeed—a sad case—but not a charity case by any means. A check arrives every month from a certain bank representing the estate of a late distinguished person. I cannot mention the name, you understand. The executors of the estate are the ones who brought Mr. O'Brien to our attention. He was quite raving at the time. He still raves a good deal."

"About what?"

"Something about a marvelous phenomenon—a baseball pitcher. I think he calls him Johnny Noonan. Anyway, this Noonan fellow, it seems, can do some mighty unnatural things with a baseball. Don't ask me what. I have no idea. I know little about that foolish game. And frankly, I could not care less."

"What about his activities here at the hospital?"

"Ah. That is a very good question. One that I am proud to answer. You see, we—that is, *I*—have developed a program compatible with the patients' backgrounds and skills. It is a wonderful innovation in the care of disturbed people. With respect to Mr. O'Brien, a former baseball person, we have given him a small workshop where he spends his time making baseballs, which we are able to sell."

"Amazing!"

"Ah. But that is not all. Mr. O'Brien has a very fertile imagination. And so we allow him to use the workshop—he calls it his laboratory—for his own personal experiments."

"Experiments?"

"Yes. He creates different kinds of baseballs out of all sorts of materials. He claims it will be a hundred years before another Johnny Noonan comes along. So, in the meantime, he thinks ordinary pitchers should have a ball that can jump under and over bats, turn corners, and stop in mid-air."

"Is that right?"

"Yes. As a matter of fact he is finishing one new one now. It is very interesting. We are all excited about it.

124

Mr. O'Brien thinks he has finally found the answer. And I must say that I am inclined to agree with him. I cannot wait to see the first tests."

"What's this new ball like?"

"Well. It looks just like a regular baseball as near as I can tell. But at its very center—and this is the interesting part—there is a bunch of Mexican jumping beans."

"Al, I think we ought to look for Johnny Noonan. There's a story in this somewhere. I can feel it."

LEONARD EVERETT FISHER, painter, illustrator, author, and educator, was born and raised in New York City. His formal art training began at the Heckscher Foundation in 1932 and was completed, after his wartime military service, at the Yale Art School, from which he received a Master of Fine Arts degree and the Winchester Fellowship. He had studied previously with Moses Soyer, Reginald Marsh, Olindo Ricci, and Serge Chermayeff. In 1950 Mr. Fisher received a Pulitzer Art Fellowship. He spent much of that year in Europe, returning home in 1951 to become dean of the Whitney School of Art in New Haven, Connecticut. He resigned from that post in 1953 and turned his attention to children's literature. Since then he has illustrated approximately two hundred children's books, about thirty of which he has written, including *The Death of "Evening Star."* He has received numerous citations, and in 1968 he was awarded the Premio Grafico for juvenile illustration by the International Book Fair, Bologna, Italy—the only American thus honored. Books containing his illustrations have been published in a variety of foreign languages and distributed throughout the world by the United States Information Agency. In addition he has designed ten United States postage stamps. Mr. and Mrs. Fisher live in Westport, Connecticut.